Heart-Stirring STORIES OF Love

LINDA EVANS SHEPHERD

Love,
Linda Evans Shepherd

BROADMAN
& HOLMAN
PUBLISHERS

Nashville, Tennessee

*Dedicated to James Kenneth (Jimmy) Evans
and his wonderful wife, Mary,
and children, Elizabeth and James Tray (J.T.)*

*Dear Brother,
Thank you for supplying us with such a colorful
childhood. Remember the flying chairs, the time you
fell off Pike's Peak, the time you drew a mustache on
my high school yearbook picture, or the time you hid in
the bushes and scared my date with tape-recorded
laughter when he rang our doorbell?
I do.
You have given me endless fodder for countless books
and articles. In fact, just wait until you see what I wrote
about you this time! (See, I was taking notes!)
Love ya,
Your Big Sis, Linda*

*Also special thanks to my assistant,
Donna Rae Manzanares.
Thanks for all your help!*

Contents

Part 1: *Love Sacrifices* 1

Part 2: *Love Encourages* 25

Part 3: *Love Grows Faith* 45

Part 4: *Love Lets Go* 73

Part 5: *Love Laughs* 99

Part 6: *Love Forgives* 117

Part 7: *Love Befriends* 145

Part 8: *Romancing Love* 171

Part 9: *God's Love* 193

Part 10: *Love Inspires* 209

Part 11: *Love through Loss* 227

Part 12: *Love Brings Joy* 247

About Linda Evans Shepherd 271

Permissions 272

Contributors 273

The best and most beautiful things in the world
cannot be seen or even touched.
They must be felt with the heart.
Helen Keller

1
Love Sacrifices

Love is the only thing you get more of
by giving it away.

Tom Wilson

A Mother's Gift

LeAnn Thieman

"I'm so glad you're coming to live with us, Aunt Emma," twelve-year-old Jane said as she placed a hand-knitted bunting into the trunk of keepsakes. Jane's mama had gone downstairs to pack the kitchen, leaving Jane to help her aunt pack sentimental items.

Jane gazed out the open window of the old two-story farmhouse and saw the roof of her own home at the far end of the cornfield. Her papa's plow sat where he had unhitched the team of horses before last night's rainstorm. Today's eastern wind carried the pounding of his hammer as he proudly finished the construction of their new home—with extra rooms for Aunt Emma.

Emma sighed. "I'm glad I'm moving in with you. This house is too big for me to be rambling around in now that I'm all alone."

Jane's face reflected the anguish she saw in her aunt. It was still hard to believe Emma's husband and four children wouldn't come racing up the steps again. They were gone forever, all dying in one week during last year's diphtheria epidemic.

Jane missed Aunt Emma's children more than anyone knew. They had been like brothers and sisters to her. As an only child, she had spent most of her life ganging up with the two girls to fend off their two older, pesky brothers. Now she usually cried as she walked home through the cornrows that had once been paths linking their lives.

"I'm really going to miss this old place though." Emma waved her hand toward the faded wallpaper and worn woodwork. "This is the only home I've known since we left the old country." Her eyes filled with tears as she hugged a baby quilt to her chest before placing the quilt in the trunk.

"Tell me again about leaving Ireland with Mama and Papa," Jane coaxed, hoping to see Aunt Emma's eyes dance as usual when she recalled that adventure.

"You've heard that story a hundred times," Emma said as she eased into the rocking chair with a bundle of children's clothes in her lap.

"But I love it!" Jane begged, "Tell me again about Mama and Papa then."

While she never gave much thought to having been adopted, Jane sometimes wondered whether that explained her relentless yearning for old family stories. She sat on the braided rug at the foot of the rocker and listened.

"Well, your mother and I were best friends—like sisters—all our lives."

Jane blurted in on cue, "That's why I call you aunt, even though we're not related!"

Emma winked and smiled.

The truth was, next to Mama and Papa, Jane loved Emma more than anyone else in the world.

"So, of course, then our husbands became best friends," Emma continued. "We did everything together, the four of us. We danced . . . ." Emma's voice trailed off and her head swayed slightly, as if in time with the music. Then her eyes danced too.

"We shared everything—good times and bad.

Your mama was there at every one of our children's births, even though she could never have one of her own." Emma took her usual pause and shook her head slowly. "There was never a woman who wanted, or deserved, a child like your mama did. She wanted a baby more than anything else on earth."

"I know," Jane whispered, then beamed, "That's why I'm so glad she got me! She calls me her 'special gift.'"

Emma took a deep breath. "So when my husband Patrick had a chance to come to a Wisconsin farm in America, it didn't take long to decide your folks would come along too. Like I said, we shared everything."

Emma rocked as she recounted the difficult journey. The storm at sea had tossed the ship for weeks. All the passengers got sick.

"Especially me," Emma moaned. "I was expecting our fifth child. If it hadn't been for your mama, I wouldn't have survived that trip. Patrick and the others were far too sick to care for me. I could tell I was about to lose the baby." She stopped to blot tears with the child's shirt she was holding. "Your mother left her own sick bed to help me. She was as sick as everyone else but stayed with me, prayed with me. . . ." Her voice trailed off again. "She was an angel. If it hadn't been for her, both the baby and I would have died then and there."

Jane rested her head on Emma's lap. "I'm so glad you made it. My life wouldn't have been the same without you."

Jane looked up into her aunt's face. This was the part of the story that was hard to repeat, so Jane said it for her. "Thanks to Mama, that baby girl was born on that old ship, all pink and pretty!" Both their faces lit up. The glow faded, however, when Jane added, "But the next day your baby went to live with the angels."

Emma only nodded, then abruptly stood and began placing the items on her lap into the trunk of treasures. Without speaking, she went to a bureau drawer and began sorting more children's clothes. Some worn items were put in a wooden crate. Others she placed reverently into the trunk.

The old wooden stairs creaked as Mama came up from the kitchen, took Jane's hand, and sat next to her on the bed.

From the bottom drawer Emma retrieved a bundle wrapped in white linen and tied with a satin bow. She took it to the bed and unwrapped it slowly. One by one she laid the tiny, white garments on the bedspread.

"These are the baptism gowns I made for each of my babies before they were born," she said softly.

Mama squeezed Jane's hand.

Emma's fingers trembled as she smoothed the fabric and straightened the lace on each delicate gown. "I stitched each one by hand and crocheted the trim myself."

Mama reached for Aunt Emma's hand and stroked it, as if silently sharing in the telling of this story.

Emma picked up the gowns one at a time. "I was going to give them to my children to keep when they grew up." She could barely speak. "This one was Colin's. This one was Shane's. This was Kathleen's. This was Margaret's."

Her tears fell onto the fifth one as she handed it to Jane. "And this one was yours."

Thoughts, memories, and old stories tumbled wildly in Jane's head. She stared into her mother's loving eyes before turning back to Emma. "What are you saying, Aunt Emma?"

Emma's voice shook. "Did you ever notice I never said that baby girl died, just that she went to live with God's angels?"

Jane nodded. "I was that baby?" Her lips curved in a hesitant smile. "And Mama and Papa were God's angels on earth!"

Now Emma nodded. "It was tradition in the old country—when someone couldn't have a baby, another family would give them one of theirs. I loved your mama so much . . . ." Her voice broke, so Mama finished the sentence.

"She and Patrick gave us the greatest gift of love."

Jane's smile widened. "Your special gift." She wrapped her arms around her Mama.

Tears flooded down Mama's cheeks as she rocked Jane in her arms. "It's as if God gave you to Papa and me for safekeeping."

Emma cried softly. "I'd have lost you with all the others."

Jane fondled the baptism gown in her hands, then embraced Emma, whispering, "Thank you."

The sound of Papa's hammering drifted through the open window. Emma smiled and her eyes danced. "Twelve years ago on that ship, I gave your folks the greatest gift. Now they share that special gift with me."

The Rich Family in Our Church

Eddie Ogan

I'll never forget Easter 1946. I was fourteen, my little sister Ocy, twelve, and my older sister Darlene, sixteen. We lived at home with our mother, and the four of us knew what it was to do without many things.

My dad had died five years before, leaving my mom with seven school kids to raise and no money. By 1946 my oldest sisters were married, and my brothers had left home.

A month before Easter, the pastor of our church announced that a special Easter offering would be taken to help a poor family. He asked everyone to save and give sacrificially.

When we got home we talked about what we could do. We decided to buy fifty pounds of potatoes and live on them for a month. This would allow us to save twenty dollars of our grocery money for the offering.

Then we thought that if we kept our electric lights turned out as much as possible and didn't listen to the radio, we'd save money on that month's electric bill. Darlene got as many house- and yard-cleaning jobs as possible, and both of us baby-sat for everyone we could. For fifteen cents, we could buy enough cotton loops to make three potholders and sell them for a dollar. We made twenty dollars on potholders.

That month was one of the best months of our lives. Every day we counted the money to see how much we saved. At night we'd sit in the dark and talk about how the poor family was going to enjoy having the money the church would give them. We had about eighty people in church, so we figured that whatever amount of money we had to give, the offering would be twenty times that much. After all, every Sunday the pastor had reminded everyone to save for the sacrificial offering.

The day before Easter, Ocy and I walked to the grocery store and got the manager to give us three crisp twenty-dollar bills and one ten-dollar bill for all of our change. We ran all the way home to show Mom and Darlene. We had never seen so much money before.

That night we were so excited we could hardly sleep. We didn't care that we wouldn't have new clothes for Easter; we had seventy dollars for the sacrificial offering. We could hardly wait to get to church!

On Sunday morning, it was pouring rain. We didn't own an umbrella, and the church was over a mile from our home, but it didn't seem to matter how wet we got. Darlene had cardboard in her shoes to fill the holes. The cardboard came apart, and her feet got wet. But as we sat proudly in church, I heard some teenagers talking about the Smith girls wearing their old dresses. I looked at them and their new clothes, and I felt rich.

When the sacrificial offering was taken, we were sitting in the second row from the front. Mom put in the ten-dollar bill, and each of us girls put in a twenty. As we walked home after church, we sang all the way. At lunch mom had a surprise for us. She had bought a dozen eggs, and we had boiled Easter eggs with our fried potatoes!

Late that afternoon the minister drove up to our house in his car. Mom went to the door, talked to him for a moment, and came back with an envelope in her hand. We asked what it was, but she didn't say a word. She opened the envelope, and out fell a wad of money—three crisp twenty-dollar bills, one ten, and seventeen ones.

Mom put the money back in the envelope. We didn't talk; we just sat there and stared at the floor. We had gone from feeling like millionaires to poor white trash.

We kids had such a happy life that we felt sorry for anyone who didn't have our mom and a house full of brothers and sisters and other kids visiting constantly. We thought it was fun to share silverware and see whether we got the fork or the spoon that night. We had two knives that we passed around to whomever needed them.

I knew we didn't have a lot of things other people had, but I'd never thought we were poor; that Easter day I found out we were. The minister had brought us the money for the poor family.

I didn't like being poor. I looked at my dress and worn-out shoes and felt so ashamed that I didn't want to go back to church. Everyone there probably already knew we were poor. I thought about school. I was in the ninth grade and at the top of my class of more than one hundred students. I wondered if the kids at school knew we were poor. I thought perhaps I should quit school because I had finished the eighth grade. That was all the law required at that time.

We sat in silence for a long time. Then it got dark, and we went to bed. All that week, we girls went to school and came home, and no one talked much.

Finally on Saturday, Mom asked, "What do you want to do with the money?"

We didn't know. We never knew we were poor.

We didn't want to go to church on Sunday, but Mom said we had to. Although it was a sunny day, we didn't talk on the way. Mom started to sing, but no one joined in, and she only sang one verse.

At church we had a missionary speaker. He talked about how churches in Africa made buildings out of sun-dried bricks, but they needed money to buy roofs. He said a hundred dollars would put a roof on a church. The minister asked, "Can't we all sacrifice to help these poor people?"

We looked at each other and smiled for the first time in a week. Mom reached into her purse and pulled out the envelope. She passed it to Darlene, Darlene gave it to me, and I handed it to Ocy. Ocy put it into the offering plate.

When the offering was counted, the minister announced that it was a little more than one hundred dollars. The missionary was excited. He hadn't expected such a large offering from our small church. He said, "You must have some rich people in this church."

Suddenly it struck us! We had given eighty-seven dollars of that "little more than one hundred dollars." We were the rich family in the church! Hadn't the missionary said so?

From then on I've never been poor again. I've always remembered how rich I am because I have Jesus.

Two Gifts

Jo Huddleston

When the film version of Margaret Mitchell's immortal *Gone with the Wind* leapt onto movie screens in glorious Technicolor, I was five years old. I was an only child and the apple of my daddy's eye. How my dad wished he, like Rhet Butler, could give his daughter a pony. However, he was barely making a living in the postdepression South. His small paycheck gave little hope of being able to give me such a lavish gift.

One day, a photographer who traveled from town to town with a pretty brown-and-white pony stopped at our door. He hawked a tempting offer: For twenty-five cents, paid in advance, I could sit on that pretty pony and have my picture taken!

My daddy was determined his little girl would have that chance, no matter that twenty-five cents was a sizable portion of his fifteen-dollar-a-week paycheck.

On that clear Saturday morning, the pony stood obediently in our front yard where the photographer talked with my parents and collected his fee. I stayed on the front porch and gazed at her in awe. I bravely imagined myself as little Bonnie Butler dressed in her finery, rushing my pony toward a jump.

As Daddy led me toward the pony, my eyes widened in growing wonder at the beautiful animal. But the closer we came, the bigger the pony seemed. When I looked up at her silver-trimmed saddle, it was like looking up at the top of a tall, straight pine tree. The little pony, who was so sweetly in my thoughts

11

only moments ago, was now standing in real life next to me. I was terrified of this immense beast.

I looked from the pony to my daddy for rescue. On his face I saw the most satisfied look I had ever seen. Instinctively, I decided I couldn't rob him of his pleasure.

Daddy helped the man put the black, fuzzy chaps on my legs while Mother tied the red bandanna at the back of my neck. The photographer put both my feet in the stirrups and turned to ready his camera and tripod. Smiling broadly, Daddy set the cowboy hat on my head, angled low over my left ear, and slid the string tight under my chin. I sat in fright, feeling I would fall off the pony and surely die.

Daddy backed away from the pony's side, and I was alone on top of the animal. The distance between me and Daddy and Mother seemed forever. Wanting to please my daddy, I took a giant step toward the Best Actress Award I would later receive at college.

I fixed a frozen smile across my face and, with white knuckles, held tightly to the reins of the lethargic pony. This was indeed brilliant acting because in the midst of my great pretending, all I wanted to do was cry.

Now more than fifty years later, Daddy is no longer living, but I can look at that black-and-white picture postcard of the smiling child on the pony and fondly remember how two gifts were given that day. My daddy and I had bonded in the delight of bringing pleasure into each other's lives.

The Love Squad

Virelle Kidder

"Oh no! Not company!" I groaned out loud the moment my car rounded the corner and our house came into full view. Normally I'd be thrilled to see four cars lined up in our driveway, but after a weeklong vigil at the hospital with a very ill child, I knew my house would be a colossal mess. "Oh well, who cares?" None of it seemed important now. Turning off the engine, I dragged myself to the front door to face the music.

"What are you doing home so soon?" my friend Julie called from the kitchen. "We weren't expecting you for another hour! We thought we'd be long gone by then." She walked toward me with a huge hug, then added softly, "How are you doin', girl?"

Was this my house? Was I dreaming? Everything looked so good. Where did these flowers come from?

Suddenly, more voices, more hugs. Lorraine, smiling and wiping beads of perspiration from her forehead, came up from the family room where she had just finished all our laundry and my entire mountain of ironing. Regina peeked into the kitchen with a little giggle, having vacuumed, polished, and dusted every room in the house. Joan, still upstairs wrestling with the boy's bunk-bed sheets, called down her hello, having brought order out of pure chaos in each of our bedrooms.

"When did you guys get here?" I plopped down exhausted on a kitchen chair. It was my last coherent sentence. Once the tears came, they came in great waves. "How come . . . how come . . . you did all this?" I cried unashamedly, every ounce of resistance gone. We had spent a week praying through a health crisis, begging God for a sense of his presence at the hospital. Instead, he laid a mantle of order, beauty, and loving care through our home with these four angels.

"Don't you worry about a thing," Lorraine said firmly. "Here's your dinner for tonight, and there is more food in the freezer." The table was set with flowers and fancy napkins, a little gift at my place. Arranged on the stove was a banquet complete with salad and dessert in the fridge.

"You rest awhile now, Virelle. We're all praying. God has everything under control. Don't you worry." One by one, my four friends left as quickly as they had come. I wandered from room to room, still sobbing from the enormity of their gift. *They must have picked every flower in their gardens,* I thought, finding beautiful arrangements in every room. And what's this? Little wrapped gifts on each bed. More tears.

It was in the living room that I found their small note under a vase of peonies. I was to have come home and find it as their only signature. Will I ever forget the words? Not even when I'm an old lady. "The Love Squad was here."

Rescued

Andria Anderson

My husband Jason had gone on business trips to Peru so often that it seemed like a normal commute. I missed him every time, of course, but I had a routine to follow. With two children, Jeremy, age four, and Susan, age six, I'd have plenty to do during the three weeks he'd be gone.

I was taking groceries into the house from the car one day, about a week after he had left, when the call came.

"Hello," I said brightly. The sunny weather had me in a good mood.

"Mrs. Johnson?" said a man's voice.

Oh, no, I thought, *not another solicitor.*

"Mrs. Johnson, this is Dave Westschire at Bellamor."

Bellamor? I wondered. Bellamor Corporation was the company Jason worked for. *Why is he calling me instead of Jason?*

I told the man, "I'm sorry, but Jason is on a trip to Peru. Since it's a sales trip for Bellamor, I'm surprised you don't already know that."

"We do know, Mrs. Johnson." His voice stopped, and I wondered what he could have to say to me.

"Mrs. Johnson, we have—" he stopped once again. "Mrs. Johnson, could you sit down, please?"

My mind froze with dread, and I sank onto a kitchen chair. "I'm sitting," I said woodenly.

"I'm sorry, ma'am, but Jason is missing. The police have been notified, but they seem to have no clues as to how to find him."

Jason? Missing? He couldn't be missing. Everyone knew he was in Peru. I hung up the phone feeling numb.

During the evening that followed, I put the children to bed as usual. But for me, the hours of darkness crept by. *Was my husband all right? Was he still alive? Oh, please let him be alive,* I prayed.

In the morning, it was all I could do to pour cereal for the children. Susan had asked what was wrong with my eyes. I made up an explanation about how they were just swollen, nothing to worry about. When the phone rang, I leaped for it.

"Yes?" I gasped. I didn't even think to say hello.

"Mrs. Johnson? The Peruvian government received a ransom note late last night," said the male voice at the other end of the connection.

Ransom note, I thought. *Ransom notes are for people who are still alive.*

"Bellamor will pay it, right?" I asked.

"Unfortunately, Mrs. Johnson, the rebel group does not want money. They want four of their members released from prison in exchange for Jason."

"Well, that should be even easier then," I said, feeling the first stirrings of hope.

There was a long silence at the other end of the line.

"What?" I asked. "What is it?"

The man, *was it Mr. Westschire again?* sighed. "No, ma'am, I'm sorry. The exchange request makes it much more complicated."

Softly, I asked, "Why?"

"The Peruvian government has a policy of non-negotiation with rebel forces. They also have a policy of never exchanging prisoners convicted of treason."

"Never?" I whispered into the phone.

"But, please, Mrs. Johnson, believe me. We are going to work as hard as we can for Jason's release. We'll offer them money, equipment, whatever they want. And we've already contacted Washington. We've asked them to apply diplomatic pressure on the government."

"Is there anything I can do?" I asked, suddenly filled with anger at people who would steal my children's father from them.

"Yes. You and as many people as you can get should start a letter-writing campaign. Write to both the Peruvian government and the United Nations. You can also contact your senator and Amnesty International."

Frantically, I searched for paper to take notes. *Who is my senator? No matter, I can find that out. What is Amnesty International? It looked like I'd be learning a whole new slate of material.*

So began weeks of frustration—not just for me, but for everyone who tried to help.

Mr. Westschire's secretary would call me about once a week to report on the company's efforts on Jason's behalf. She'd tell me what the embassy in Peru was doing and what the company had offered the rebels this time.

I'd tell her about the letters that the group at my church had written or what the Amnesty International contact had reported. "Yes," I told her one time, "my family is helping with Susan and Jeremy, but Jason's folks can't stand to hear about the negotiations any more. They said not to tell them anything unless he's on his way home."

I always told her to pass my thanks along for the continued paychecks.

The weeks dragged into months. For every positive development, two setbacks would break my heart. If the rebels agreed to some terms, the government didn't. If the government responded to international pressure, the rebels resisted.

I told Susan and Jeremy that their daddy's trip was just longer this time. I kept their lives as normal as possible. If Susan overheard a phone conversation, I explained it away as best I could.

Never, in all those months, was Jason allowed to call or write to his family.

Occasionally the rebels sneaked letters into the U.S. Embassy restating their demands and reporting that Jason was healthy. We wondered what a rebel's idea of *healthy* was.

I had no way to tell if my letters, addressed to the rebel group in care of the embassy, ever reached him. I prayed that he could feel our concern, that he could keep believing we were all working toward his release.

In October, after seven months of disappointments, another call came from Mr. Westschire.

"Mrs. Johnson, we at Bellamor know how worried you have been. And I wanted to tell you of a new development."

I didn't dare let my heart hope. There had been too many dashed prospects in the past.

Mr. Westschire continued, "Mr. Bellamor is going to Peru. He wants to talk to the people there himself. The board has empowered him to offer anything that might get Jason released."

I couldn't believe what I'd just heard. *The president and CEO of the whole company is going to go get Jason now?* Despite my best efforts, a tiny seed of hope did begin to grow.

The nervous tension I felt was like the first week of the kidnapping all over again. Any phone call might be news of Jason coming home. I took care of my children by habit. I couldn't sleep, and I couldn't eat. After eight days I was exhausted.

"Mrs. Johnson!" Mr. Westschire's excited voice greeted me on the phone then. "Jason is on his way home. His flight is due at the international terminal at nine o'clock tonight."

I just cried.

I didn't quite dare to tell the children—for fear that Jason wouldn't really arrive as promised. So I arranged for a sitter and went to the airport alone.

The scene at the airport was so subdued. Few people were around at that hour. But I thought the TV station should have reporters there. I thought the newspaper should have a photographer to catch the moment. After seven months of frightened waiting, my husband was coming home!

The flight was only half an hour late. As I watched people disembark, I suddenly wondered if I would recognize him. And would he remember me? I touched my hair. I had cut it short, and he wouldn't know about that.

Then I spotted a familiar figure. I'd know that walk anywhere. It didn't matter that he had a beard. It didn't matter how thin he was. This was my Jason!

We grabbed each other in the tightest hug we could hold. The tears on our faces ran together as we kissed.

"I thought that government would never give up those prisoners," I said to my beloved husband.

Jason pulled away and looked at me strangely. "Didn't they tell you?" he said.

"Tell me what?" I asked.

"How I got released," he answered.

I just looked at him, confused.

"The government refused to exchange any prisoners. They even refused to talk to any more Americans," Jason explained.

He stopped and looked in my eyes. Then he said, very softly, "Mr. Bellamor, he—" Jason stopped again, swallowing back more tears. "Mr. Bellamor . . . took my place, Jennifer."

I stood staring at him.

"He said it was his business that got me captured, so it was his business to get me released. He's staying there, Jennifer, as a prisoner of the rebels. He stayed so I could come home."

A Generous Heart

Natalie Nicole Gilbert

The ad was short and sweet but had all the signs of a good find. The older man was looking for something that would hold up for a while and be easy enough for him to play. He called and made arrangements to stop in later that night after taking his grandson to baseball practice.

The apartment was situated on a busy highway, squeezed between a gas station and a department store. With ease the old Cadillac found its way to the right apartment. Before he even had a chance to knock, a young man opened the door and gave him a warm smile as a welcome.

"Hi, I'm John, the one you spoke to on the phone." He extended his hand, which was accepted for a firm shake by the man. "I think you'll like what you see."

John led him through the rather empty living room to a back room. There it sat, in an open case, a beautiful acoustic guitar whose neck and body had been well polished and maintained. This was just what the older man was looking for.

"Would you like to play it to see how it sounds?" John asked.

"Me? Play? I don't know that I could just yet. I'm hoping to learn, but right now I'm not even sure how to hold a pick, son," the older man responded.

"Well, to give you an idea of its potential I could play something for you, if you'd like. I spent a few years taking lessons and used this guitar for some concerts and campfire retreats."

"I think I'd enjoy that. Take a stab at it, young man."

The look of joy on John's face was unmistakable as he picked up his old friend and began to play a medley. It was obvious that he knew the guitar well, for his fingers flowed with ease over every chord. He hummed a light tune as he journeyed through his short solo. The older man smiled at his enthusiasm and zeal for the instrument. As the music found its end, the visitor let a sigh of compliment pass his lips.

"Can I ask you a question, John?"

"Certainly!" he smiled.

"Why would someone with your talent be selling a guitar? Did someone give you an instrument nicer than this one?"

John's smile deflated. "Well, sir, fact is, my wife and I need the money that selling this guitar will give us. You see, we're expecting a child soon, and what we make won't provide for the added expenses just now. Truth is, I hate to see this beauty go." John looked to the floor, acknowledging his longing to see a different answer to the current need.

"But, I have another little beauty coming," John stated with a smile, "and she's worth the sacrifice."

The older man gave it a moment's consideration before making his offer, "Well, son, I'm ready to write you a check."

"That's great! I sure appreciate your coming by tonight. Your timing couldn't be better. Little Sara is due in just a matter of weeks now. I have some guitar books I used when I first took some lessons. Would you like me to toss those in?"

"I don't think they'd do me much good, young man," the older man offered as he scribbled his signature on the check.

John was puzzled. "I can tell you they're pretty easy to work with. I didn't know much about guitars when I used them, and I think they helped me a good bit."

"I'm sure the books are good, but I won't have a guitar to practice on so they wouldn't help me much."

With confusion, John stumbled over his words, "You're not . . . you don't want . . . . But, you're giving me a check for the guitar? . . . I don't understand."

The old man grinned, "I'm paying you to keep the guitar. It belongs in your hands, young man. No one else knows that guitar the way you do. No one else would play it as well as you do. But I do believe the good Lord had in mind for me to give you this check to help you." The man handed him the check.

"I was once in your shoes, I know your need, and I've seen a piece of your heart today, knowing that you'd be willing to give up your most prized possession for your family's needs. I admire that, and I'm happy to reward you for your willingness to sacrifice."

John was humbled and silent. "But can't I offer you something?"

With contentment in his voice, the old man made his request, "Just love that little girl, and never let your wife wonder about where your affections are."

With that said, the older man turned to make his way to the door. John took a quick moment to reflect on this man's generosity as he walked with him.

"I don't know how to thank you for what you've just done."

"You already have, son."

The man got in his car and drove off, without glancing back. John watched him as far as he could from his front door. As he pushed the door closed, he took a look at the check the man had written him, and his eyes began to water as he looked at the amount. The day had started with a hope, and his hope had been answered with a gift even greater than he could have imagined.

2
Love Encourages

Old or young or long or short
Or plump or thin, it's clear:
All arms are just exactly right
For hugging someone dear!

Bonnie Compton Hanson

Love That Blossoms

Nanette Thorsen-Snipes

Curiously, the warmth of the spring day felt good on my skin. I fought back the veil of tears that blurred the dogwood trees lining the hospital grounds. Everything around me seemed to burst with life while I felt cold, alone, and defeated.

With a sinking feeling I opened my car door and drove to the florist. I knew I had to do this for my mother. She had always said, "Give me flowers while I can enjoy them." As I opened the door to the florist's shop, I was met by a profusion of color mingled with the scent of fresh roses. What a contrast with the bare hospital room I had just left! My mother had been in the hospital for more than two weeks, her yearlong struggle with lung cancer nearly at an end. And I wanted more than anything to see her smile once more.

I walked between the potted daisies, pausing to finger the petals. They still shimmered with water droplets, and I couldn't help thinking of how vibrant they seemed. The shelves below them were lined with pottery exploding with philodendron. Everything seemed blessed with life and the will to live. I turned and faced the sunlight streaming through the window, hoping it would drive out the ache in my throat. I breathed in deeply, then glanced up at the top shelf. There I saw an old-fashioned yellow sprinkling can brimming with lavender daisies. As I lifted it from the shelf, the flowers practically danced.

"Can I help you?" a voice behind me asked. I turned to face a woman I didn't know. She must have sensed the pain in my heart or seen the tears in my eyes because her eyes were full of compassion. "I-I want something pretty for my mother," I managed to say. "She's dying."

Without so much as a word, the woman, who worked daily nurturing life within the flower shop, walked forward. Her deep brown eyes melted into a mixture of pain, understanding, and love as she gently placed her arms around me.

In that unexpected embrace, I felt God's love as he welcomed me into his arms, surrounding me and protecting me from the pain. At once, the familiar words of Jesus spoke clearly to me, "By this shall all men know that ye are my disciples, if ye have love one to another" (John 13:35 KJV).

There in that flower shop God met me, a defeated and lonely person trying to muddle through a tragedy without him. But through his love, he sent someone to meet me in my sorrow. I thank God every day for this woman who allowed the love of Jesus to work through her. My prayer is that I follow her example and meet others where they are, freely offering the love of Jesus.

From the Lips of Babes

Renee Coates Scheidt

"Don't cry, Mama. We'll help you clean it up," my eleven- and eight-year-old daughters said as they threw their arms around my waist. We stared in disbelief at the vegetable soup splattered over the stove, countertops, walls, and floor.

The pressure-relief plug on the cooker had become clogged. When I took off the top, the built-up pressure flung bits of tomatoes, potatoes, carrots, peas, and beef everywhere. The mess would take a long time to clean up, and my plans for supper were blown away as well. Only a few hours before, the day had gotten off to a bad start when my coffeemaker had overflowed.

Stay calm, Renee, I told myself. No big deal. You can handle this.

The pressure was building, however. The day before, my oldest child, Nicole, had declared that she was ready to go back to school after being sick. I worried about her all morning, so I went to school and had lunch with her. I was to be gone that evening to lead a young widows seminar in a neighboring town, and I had to make sure she was OK.

I raced home from the seminar that night, anxious to check on Nicole. Blue lights appeared in my rearview mirror and headed toward me.

Oh, no! I thought. How fast was I going? The unsympathetic officer let me know exactly how fast as he wrote the ticket. Through hot tears, I drove home.

A sick daughter, a speeding ticket, coffee all over the floor, and vegetable soup flung throughout the kitchen—all within a few short hours. What else could go wrong? It was only nine o'clock on what should have been a leisurely Saturday morning, and I felt like a pressure cooker myself, ready to explode.

Together, Nicole, Tara, and I cleaned up the mess. "Girls, you go play now," I said. "I'll finish up here."

Several minutes later I heard their voices calling, "Mama come in here. We have something to show you."

Dropping the dishcloth, I headed toward the sound of their voices. They met me in the hallway with eyes aglow. "Go look on your bed, Mama. We made something for you."

At the center of the bed, I spied a note written on blue construction paper atop a tissue-wrapped package. The tissue fell off when I picked it up, revealing a small bag Tara had made from scraps of material. Then I read the note little hands had printed: "'And we know that in all things God works for the good of those who love him' (Rom. 8:28 NIV). So, Mom, keep on trusting in him, and you'll do fine because he did this for a purpose. Love, Nicole and Tara."

It was the verse I had often quoted to them after their father's death by suicide eight years earlier—the verse we had clung to in those dark days when I didn't know how we would make it; the verse that had been the anchor of our souls as we made our way through the valley of the shadow of death.

Tears flowed in frustration and joy: frustration at myself for allowing circumstances to get the best of me and joy in seeing the impact God had in my children's lives. Perhaps things weren't as bad as they had appeared earlier. Perhaps the trying circumstances of the recent hours were worth the prize. For what greater joy can there be than to see God's Word springing forth in the lives of our children, giving back what we have given them?

A Thankful Heart

Nanette Thorsen-Snipes

I stood at the kitchen sink that day in 1994, shelling hard-boiled eggs. It was hard to be thankful. Everyone I knew was preparing Thanksgiving dinner, but my plans had been canceled.

Just two days before, my teenage daughter Jamie had undergone an appendectomy. Jamie's operation, coupled with the anniversary of Benny's (my former husband) suicide, allowed depression to seep in at the edges of my life much like warm water seeped between the egg and eggshell I held.

Our church, learning that we wouldn't be able to spend Thanksgiving with my son and his wife, had brought us a small turkey. Shelling another egg, I remembered learning of Benny's suicide in a county jail after he'd tried to kill his wife; it was the same haunting reason I'd left him so many years before. He had tried to kill me.

Every year I planned to be busy enough so that I didn't have time to remember his suicide. This year was different. Outside my kitchen window, drops of rain pattered the deck. The sky loomed steel gray and the wind from the west brought more rain. Depression played like a dirge at the edges of my mind.

"Mama," Jamie said, "would you take this off my arm?" I walked into the living room and snipped the hospital band from her wrist. I was angry that my husband had time to sit down and read the paper. I'd stayed awake most of the previous night and was exhausted. *The least he could do is help,* I thought.

Two days earlier Jamie had come out of her bedroom doubled over in pain. She managed to say, "My stomach hurts." Thinking it was nothing more than a virus, I helped her to the couch and covered her with a quilt.

As the minutes passed, Jamie's pain became more intense. She had no fever or nausea—at first. When the pain moved to her right side, I sped her to the emergency room.

On the way, she started vomiting, and her temperature rose. However, after the doctors checked her out, they insisted on sending her home. With a mother's intuition, I refused and called my family doctor. He arrived within the hour and correctly diagnosed her. Nine hours after we'd entered the hospital, Jamie had an emergency appendectomy.

I sliced another egg and removed the yolk while I fought back tears. *What's wrong with me?* I wondered. Unbidden, the memory of my former husband raced back.

I saw myself as I had stood at Benny's casket, holding our oldest son's hand. I looked down at the deep lines etched on Benny's face. He had a full beard now and it was spiced with gray. He had aged in the years we'd been apart, yet he was only forty—in the prime of his life. Why did he commit suicide?

Years before alcohol took its toll on him, I urged Benny to go to church. I finally gave up, and our lives spiraled downward. I remembered how his personality had changed; his hostility had grown along with my fear. That same fear closed around me while I stood in my kitchen. I could almost see Benny once more lock my bedroom door, take down the box of bullets, load the gun . . . .

With the memory fresh as the day it happened twenty years before, my heart and head pounded. I steadied myself at the sink. Tears gathered. I wiped one from my cheek and called my neighbor, Donna. "Do you have anything for a headache?" I asked, trying to keep my voice from quivering.

"No," she said cheerily, "but I have to go out. I'll get you something."

My voice cracked. "That's OK, I need to get out," I said. "This has been an awful day for me." I hung up the phone. Nothing had gone right.

Thanksgiving? I wasn't thankful for anything.

I drove to the store, my nose still red from crying. I felt so exhausted, so tired. I wondered how I'd ever make Thanksgiving come together for my husband and children. I knew I should talk to God, but I was wrapped in self-pity and didn't have the energy. By the time I got home, I just wanted to crawl in bed.

Pulling into the carport, I noticed a pot of gaily wrapped lavender daisies at my back door. Jamie is so well loved, I thought gratefully. My daughter's friends had brought flowers and teddy bears all day to cheer her up. I set the flowers on the table in my kitchen.

To my surprise, a piece of paper nestled in the flowerpot bore my name. "His strength is perfect when our strength is gone," it read. As I turned the paper over, I realized it was from Donna. The heaviness in my heart lifted.

Of course, I thought, *Donna's right. God's strength is perfect. I can do all things through him who gives me strength.*

I fingered the lavender petals. Why did I give in to self-pity when I had so much to be thankful for? I bowed my head. "Thank you, Lord," I said, "for caring so much about me to send Donna . . . ."

When I returned to the sink, my husband stood there stuffing the eggs. The smell of roasting turkey permeated the room. He placed his arms around me and kissed my cheek. Even the rain had stopped, and the sun peeked from behind a gray cloud. I could feel God's peace encompassing me, and my heart overflowed with thanksgiving for a friend and a husband who cared enough to express their love.

A Gift of a Day

Barbara Vogelgesang

My dad was an old-fashioned, quiet man. He worked hard and loved his family completely. He was creative and loved to draw and paint but had to leave those pursuits undeveloped to earn a living to feed his wife and two girls. Dad spent most of his days driving a fuel oil truck through some rough neighborhoods in Brooklyn. It wasn't safe and it wasn't easy, but he remained a caring and sensitive man.

Dad and I were very close. I could share my dreams and schemes with him. I always felt he'd support me. My mom was the take-charge, practical, aggressive type. She and I just didn't click. So when I broke up with my first love, it was Dad I went to for comfort. Mom had said, "It's nothing. No one marries the first boy they date. Besides, you are only a junior in high school, much too young to be tied down to one boy. Life has many more adventures ahead for you."

Looking back, that was true, although at the time my heart was aching. There is nothing like the pain of first love lost.

Every morning my dad dropped me off at my bus stop on his way to work. The day after I broke up with my boyfriend, I wasn't looking forward to getting on the school bus and seeing my ex-boyfriend. I actually felt physically ill. As we got closer, the feeling got worse. Suddenly I noticed Dad was picking up speed and passing right by the bus stop. Before I could ask, he said, "It seems to me you need a day off, and I could use some help on the truck today. I'll call school when we get to the garage."

What a wonderful dad! He made me feel so special and so loved that day. He listened as I cried and worked through my teenage emotions. He didn't give much advice, just kept showing me and telling me how much I was loved. We shared his lunch and an ice cream in the cab of his truck.

I'll never forget that day. It was a gift my dad gave to me. He knew just what I needed. The time between the teen years and adulthood is difficult for both parent and child. I was blessed to have a father who knew all he had to do was give me his love, and the only way to do that was with his time.

Manicotti

Georgia E. Burkett

"Manicotti, Mother? I never heard of it."

"Neither did I, until I saw this," she replied, showing me a tempting magazine advertisement. "It looks delicious. Would you make some for me?"

I had come to clean mother's trailer, hoping to finish the job that same day. Ravaged by cancer, she could no longer clean or cook for herself. Nevertheless, she stubbornly refused to leave her beloved "Tin Can" to live with me. Privacy was one of the last assets Mother managed to retain, and she was determined not to lose it. So I helped her as much as she would allow.

But today I don't have time to make manicotti, I complained silently as Mother babbled on. *I don't even know how to cook it. I'll have to run to the market for hamburger, and where on earth do I find manicotti? Still, if it will tempt her appetite, I'll have to try.*

To my surprise, in the market I found manicotti stacked with all the other types of macaroni. Cooking directions on the box seemed simple enough. "Sure," I told myself. "I can fix this and still do mother's cleaning."

Later, in Mother's pocket-sized kitchen, I boiled the tube-shaped manicotti while she watched intently. "Not too long," she protested. "The recipe says just until limp."

Rolling my eyes heavenward, I groaned inwardly, *Mother, I can read.* But as I tried to stuff the spicy hamburger mixture into one of the slippery manicotti, it slipped out of my fingers, skid across the counter, and shot across the floor, landing square in front of Mother's feet.

"Whoa!" she cried. "That one must be alive. I never saw macaroni act like that before."

We both absolutely dissolved in laughter. It was one of those times when one laugh seems to generate another. What fun we had recapturing that crazy episode of the catapulting manicotti.

I patiently stuffed the rest of the manicotti with extra care, poured a jar of tomato sauce over the lot, then put them in the oven.

The aroma of their baking was just the thing to whet Mother's jaded appetite.

"They look just like the picture," she declared at noon as we sat at her tiny kitchen table eating our new treat. "Aren't they good? I'm so glad you made them. There's even enough for my dinner tomorrow."

The manicotti were good. Sweeter, though, was my pleasure in knowing that I had provided something Mother enjoyed eating. I could almost imagine God smiling down on us, blessing our sweet fellowship together.

Housework could wait, for Mother's time on earth was short. And I was determined to never again let anything spoil our last precious moments together.

All the Good Things

Helen P. Mrosla

He was in the third grade class I taught at Saint Mary's School in Morris, Minnesota. All thirty-four of my students were dear to me, but Mark Eklund was one in a million. Very neat in appearance, he had that happy-to-be-alive attitude that made even his occasional mischievousness delightful.

Mark also talked incessantly. I tried to remind him again and again that talking without permission was not acceptable. What impressed me so much, though, was his sincere response every time I had to correct him for misbehaving. "Thank you for correcting me, Sister!" I didn't know what to make of it at first, but before long I became accustomed to hearing it many times a day.

One morning my patience was growing thin when Mark talked once too often. I made a novice-teacher's mistake. I looked at Mark and said, "If you say one more word, I am going to tape your mouth shut!"

It wasn't ten seconds later when Chuck blurted out, "Mark is talking again." I hadn't asked any of the students to help me watch Mark, but since I had stated the punishment in front of the class, I had to act on it.

I remember the scene as if it had occurred this morning. I walked to my desk, very deliberately opened the drawer, and took out a roll of masking tape. Without saying a word, I proceeded to Mark's desk, tore off two pieces of tape, and made a big *X* with them over his mouth. I then returned to the front of the room.

As I glanced at Mark to see how he was doing, he

winked at me. That did it! I started laughing. The entire class cheered as I walked back to Mark's desk, removed the tape, and shrugged my shoulders. His first words were, "Thank you for correcting me, Sister."

At the end of the year, I was asked to teach junior-high math. The years flew by, and before I knew it Mark was in my classroom again. He was more handsome than ever and just as polite. Since he had to listen carefully to my instruction in the "new math," he no longer talked as much.

One Friday things just didn't feel right. We had worked hard on a new concept all week, and I sensed that the students were growing frustrated with themselves and edgy with one another. I had to stop this crankiness before it got out of hand. So I asked them to list the names of the other students in the room on two sheets of paper, leaving a space between each name. Then I told them to think of the nicest thing they could say about each of their classmates and write it down.

It took the remainder of the class period to finish the assignment, but as the students left the room, each one handed me his or her paper. Chuck smiled. Mark said, "Thank you for teaching me, Sister. Have a good weekend."

On Saturday I wrote down the name of each student on a separate sheet of paper, and I listed what everyone else had said about that individual. On Monday I gave each student his or her list. Some of the lists ran two pages. Before long, the entire class was smiling. "Really?" I heard whispered. "I never knew that meant anything to anyone!" "I didn't know others liked me so much!"

No one ever mentioned those papers in class again. I never knew if they discussed them after class or with their parents, but it didn't matter. The exercise had accomplished its purpose. The students were happy with themselves and one another again.

That group of students moved on. Several years later, after I had returned from a vacation, my parents met me at the airport. As we were driving home, Mother asked the usual questions about the trip: how the weather was, and about my experiences in general. There was a slight lull in the conversation. Mother gave Dad a sideways glance and simply said, "Dad?"

My father cleared his throat. "The Eklunds called last night," he began.

"Really?" I said. "I haven't heard from them for several years. I wonder how Mark is."

Dad responded quietly. "Mark was killed in Vietnam," he said. "The funeral is tomorrow, and his parents would like it if you would attend." To this day I can still point to the exact spot on I-494 where Dad told me about Mark.

I had never seen a serviceman in a military coffin before. Mark looked so handsome, so mature. All I could think at that moment was, *Mark, I would give all the masking tape in the world if only you could talk to me.*

The church was packed with Mark's friends. Chuck's sister sang "The Battle Hymn of the Republic." Why did it have to rain on the day of the funeral? It was difficult enough at the graveside. The pastor said the usual prayers, and the bugler played taps.

One by one, those who loved Mark took a last walk by the coffin and sprinkled it with holy water.

I was the last one to bless the coffin. As I stood there, one of the soldiers who had acted as a pallbearer came up to me. "Were you Mark's math teacher?" he asked. I nodded as I continued to stare at the coffin. "Mark talked about you a lot," he said.

After the funeral, most of Mark's former classmates headed to Chuck's farmhouse for lunch. Mark's mother and father were there, obviously waiting for me. "We want to show you something," his father said, taking a wallet out of his pocket. "They found this on Mark when he was killed. We thought you might recognize it."

Opening the billfold, he carefully removed two worn pieces of notebook paper that had obviously been taped, folded, and refolded many times. I knew without looking that the papers were the ones on which I had listed all the good things each of Mark's classmates had said about him. "Thank you so much for doing that," Mark's mother said. "As you can see, Mark treasured it."

Mark's classmates started to gather around us. Chuck smiled rather sheepishly and said, "I still have my list. It's in the top drawer of my desk at home." John's wife said, "John asked me to put his in our wedding album." "I have mine too," Marilyn said. "It's in my diary." Then Vicki, another classmate, reached into her pocketbook, took out her wallet, and showed her worn and frazzled list to the group. "I carry this with me at all times," Vicki said without batting an eyelash. "I think we all saved our lists."

That's when I finally sat down and cried. I cried for Mark and for all his friends who would never see him again.

Special Stockings

Andria Anderson

November 16 brought horrific news. My father had burned to death in the crash of a small commuter airplane, downed by electric wires in a thunderstorm.

Thanksgiving with just my sister Debi, my mother, and me had been a trial. I was glad, even if guiltily so, to get out of that house and back to college. But now I was back home for Christmas, and grief hung heavy in the air, resting on my mom's sagging shoulders. How Debi and I wished we could ease her burden.

Even though we girls always hung stockings on the fireplace mantle, this Christmas Eve we decided to forgo the tradition so my mom would have one less duty to perform. After all, we were too old anyway. Debi was fourteen, and I was twenty. But after Debi and I talked about it, we decided to fill our own stockings and maybe make one up for Mom.

What would we use to make a stocking for Mom? After all, her socks would be way too small. After a quick brainstorming session, Debi and I hit on the perfect solution; we'd hang a pair of Mom's panty hose!

It was a trick to get a pair out of her room while she was in the bathroom, and they were a bit difficult to hang on the mantle. When we dropped the traditional orange into one of the toes, let me tell you, it was a s-t-r-e-t-c-h! This leg of the panty hose now reached to the floor where the orange came to rest. Trying not to giggle too loudly, Debi put another orange in the other leg.

We laughed at this pair of oranges now tethered to our fireplace. We racked our brains for things with which to fill this stocking. Small gifts we had planned to place under the tree were called into stocking-stuffer duty. The panty hose drooped further and still had plenty of space left. Next we took candies from around the house. Bulging at all angles, the sagging panty hose begged for more. For an hour we wrapped items from all over the house. The panty hose looked like Godzilla's mother had used them, but they were finally full.

The next morning Mom was understandably reluctant to face the day, her first Christmas in twenty-six years without her beloved by her side. Debi and I were trying to keep straight faces while we waited for her to enter the living room. At first she didn't really look at the fireplace. But when she did look, she did a double take. Debi and I couldn't help cracking smiles. As she walked over to the lumpy legs of those panty hose, she began to laugh.

Here were her own panty hose holding half of our household goods. They stretched into a gargantuan size as the nails strained to hold the weight of the gifts. In the midst of green and red decorations, Mom's light tan nylons had expanded to cover the entire fireplace.

We laughed our way through opening all those gifts. Each one had to be wiggled and jiggled out of four feet of stretchy, clingy material. We might be missing our father, but our love for each other had—uh—stretched to cover the occasion.

3
Love Grows Faith

Fear knocked on the door.
Faith answered.
No one was there.

Folk Proverb

The China Terror

Jack Cavanaugh

Gladys Aylward, a British woman, wanted to be an actress, but God had other plans. He chose to take her to China as a missionary.

Once in China, all Gladys was allowed to do was to run a foot-inspection station. But that at least got her into the territory so she could talk to the people she met.

One day, just as the foot-inspection station was about to open, a man came in waving an official-looking piece of red paper. The official said, "This is a summons. You must come with me."

Gladys asked, "Why?"

"The prison warden has sent for you. There is a riot in the prison, and you must go there immediately."

"You must have the wrong person. I'm sorry there is a riot in the prison, but there is nothing I can do about it."

The official said, "You *must* come!"

Gladys's assistant looked at the paper and told her, "This is official. You *must* go."

Gladys said, "This is nonsense, obviously a mistake." She turned to her assistant. "Go with this man. Find out what this is about, then come back and tell me."

Hesitantly, her assistant set down his broom and started to leave with the official. But when the official turned right, the assistant split to the left and ran away as fast as he could.

It wasn't long before the official found that he was alone in his trek back to the prison. The official returned and told Gladys, "You *must* come with me now!"

Reluctantly, Gladys agreed.

Before the prison was even in sight, she could hear the most awful sounds of human agony. At the prison wall she found the warden and his guards huddled together in fright.

On the other side of the wall, she heard blood-curdling screams and moans. She knew terrible things were happening in the riot.

The warden said, "I'm glad you have come."

"You gave me no choice," she said. "I can't imagine why you would send for me. What do you want me to do?"

"I want you to go inside the prison and stop the riot."

Stunned, she said, "Send in your guards."

"My guards are too frightened to go in. It's too dangerous in there."

"What do you expect *me* to do?"

The warden said, "Are you not the woman who has been telling everyone in the region that you have the living God inside of you and that in a time of trouble he will come and protect you?"

Gladys nodded. With a silent prayer, she said, "Let me in."

The warden opened the door, then slammed and locked it behind her. She found herself in a long, dark, empty corridor. She worked her way down the corridor and came out into a courtyard.

As she started to walk through the courtyard, she saw bodies lying everywhere. She stumbled and looked down at a poor departed soul who lay at her feet. Then she saw a man across the courtyard with a horrid-looking machete. He was playing a very vicious game with the other prisoners—the kind of game in which his victims knew when they had been tagged.

The men ran this way, then that. As they circled around, they began to run straight for her. Suddenly they parted, and she was left standing face to face with the man with the machete in his hand.

God always gives us exactly what we need when we need it, and what this man needed right then was a mother.

Gladys put her hands on her hips and said, "Just what do you think you're doing?" She held out her hand to the slasher. "You give me that knife right now!"

The man took the machete, turned it around, and handed it to Gladys. By then she had everyone's attention. She said, "All of you! Get out here! Form a line."

They came out and formed a line. She tried to find out what had happened, but none of the prisoners would talk, so she said, "You, you, and you. Get over in that corner!" *(Mothers love corners.)* "You decide what happened and come back and tell me. And the rest of you, clean up this mess."

At that point, Gladys realized that the mess consisted of pieces of bodies strewn around the place. When the three men came back from their corners, they told her what had happened. It seems they were given that knife once a day to fix their food. An argument over whose turn it was to use the knife had triggered the riot.

Gladys went on to discover that the men were cooped up all day, and the only thing they ever got to do was to fix their own food with that knife.

Suddenly, she heard a sound behind her. The warden and his guards appeared with their guns. The warden said, "I'll take it from here."

Gladys turned on him with that knife and said, "What do you think you are doing? These men have nothing to do! No wonder you have problems like this! I'll give you one month. When I come back here, these men better have jobs to do, they better be productive, or you will have to deal with me!"

The warden accepted her challenge. *(He wouldn't dare ignore it.)* After that, Gladys returned to the prison often. She taught the prisoners about God's love for them. They listened because they had seen what God's love could do. This was the start of Gladys's prison work in China. It was a work that changed many lives with the power of God's love, simply because Gladys Aylward trusted God to protect her as she walked through a prison riot.

How Big Is God?

Linda Evans Shepherd

I was speaking to a Sunday school class of wiggling five-year-olds, when Jon, a little blond-haired boy, raised his hand. "How big is God?" he asked.

Perched in my too-tiny chair, I smoothed my hands across my blue skirt and looked down at my young charges who were sitting in a semicircle at my feet. "He's as big as you can imagine," I answered.

Jon's eyebrows shot beneath his shiny bangs. He asked, "Is he as big as a camel?"

"Yes," I smiled. "God is bigger than a camel. He created camels."

Jon looked puzzled. "Is he bigger than a giraffe?"

"Even bigger!" I assured him.

In frustration, Jon gestured his arms widely, "Is He bigger than the whole world?"

"Yes," I laughed. "God created the whole world."

Jon folded his arms across his red sweater vest; his voice sounded stern. "Then how can God fit into my heart?"

The children stared up at me with quizzical eyes. I took a deep breath. "That's a hard one," I admitted. "But let me ask you a question, Jon. How big is your love for your mom and dad?"

Jon held his hands a foot apart. "About this big," he responded matter-of-factly.

"But your heart is smaller than that. How can you fit all that love in there?"

Jon frowned. "I don't know."

I leaned forward, my eyes holding his gaze. "The way God fits into our hearts is the same way the love for our moms and dads fits into our hearts. If you invite God into your heart, he'll find room to grow as he fills your heart with a love for him."

Trust Me!

Lauraine Snelling

One hot summer afternoon I was sitting in my office in our new mountain valley home. I stared out my window over the tree-covered hills, contemplating a book I was working on.

It was only 3:30 in the afternoon, and I was making a mental list of writing accomplishments I hoped to complete before my husband Wayne came home for dinner.

The ringing of the phone jarred my thoughts. I was delighted to hear the voice of my best friend Barbara, who manages the hotel where Wayne works as a maintenance man.

Barb sounded worried. "I thought you should know. Wayne's having trouble breathing. I've tried to get him to go to the hospital, but he won't go. He says he's fine. He says he's just having trouble dealing with this hundred-degree heat."

"I hope he's right," I said. "He's been having trouble breathing all week. I tried to get him to go to the doctor, but he refused."

"I'll keep an eye on him," Barb said. "I'll call you later."

It was hard to concentrate on my work as I worried about Wayne. I began to think about the last few months. He had insisted on the move to this mountain town in California. I hadn't wanted to move so soon after our last move, but I felt as if God had coaxed me to pull out the packing boxes once again. Each time I balked God seemed to ask me, *Are you going to trust me?*

At 5:30 the phone rang again. This time I could hear a woman screaming in the background. Barb sounded frantic. "He's not breathing! I don't know what to do. I'm calling you to ask you to pray because I can't!"

No, Lord, no! Don't do this to me. Don't do this to Wayne! Please!

Barb said, "Hang on the line. I'm going to try to get 911."

I prayed the only prayer my frightened mind could muster under the circumstances. *Lord, help Wayne!*

As I prayed, two male guests at the hotel heard the screams. I could hear them run to the scene and shout, "He's having a heart attack!" I could hear as they fell to their knees and begin administering CPR, pushing against Wayne's chest and breathing into his mouth. I could hear them as they worked. "I'm not getting anything," one said.

"I think he's dead," the other said as he continued his efforts.

I heard the approaching sirens and the ambulance screech to a halt. I heard the hotel doors clatter open as the paramedics ran into the lobby.

One of the paramedics shouted, "There's nothing here. No heart, no pulse, nothing!"

I sucked in my breath as reality hit me. Clinically, Wayne was dead.

It's funny. It was if I had been prepared for this moment. For months I had felt God's gentle whisper, *Will you trust me?* I'd respond, *Yes, for who else is there?*

Even then, although I felt alone, I knew I wasn't.

A voice that was picked up over the phone line brought me back to the drama. It was the voice of one of the paramedics. "It's thready, but I'm getting his heartbeat back!"

I awakened with hope. *Lord, please, help Wayne! I'm not ready to be a widow.*

Barbara's voice broke through, "OK, they've got him on oxygen and a ventilator. They're transporting him to the hospital. How fast can you get here?"

"As soon as I can get dressed and down the mountain," I said.

When I arrived at the hospital, Barb and the doctor were waiting. The doctor said, "Wayne's on life support and unresponsive. I have no idea how it's going to go. Because he was without oxygen for so long, even if he comes out of it, he could be paralyzed and have considerable brain damage."

I slipped into Wayne's room. He was hooked to a vent. Two IVs were jammed into his arms. His face was ghastly gray against his white hair.

As I sat by his bed and held his hand, I continued to pray, "Lord, you can take Wayne to heaven, but please don't let him be a vegetable."

Somehow, I felt God's comfort. *Will you trust me?*

The next morning, Wayne was still totally paralyzed because the doctors had put him on a drug to keep him from fighting the ventilator. One of the doctors said, "I'm very concerned. Wayne is not moving, and he's not responsive to pain."

We waited. At two o'clock that afternoon the nurse told me that Wayne was starting to come out of it. When I learned he had squeezed her hand, I began to see hope. Every time he moved his hands or feet, swallowed, or followed commands, I rejoiced. Each new response was cause for celebration. He could have been paralyzed, but that didn't happen, and he had no brain damage.

Today Wayne is home and on total disability. Understandably, he's still struggling with both the physical and emotional aspects of what happened to him. But as for me, I am learning to trust God on a deeper level. I can see God had even prepared Wayne's rescuers, putting them at the right place at the right time. Wayne would have never survived the wait for the ambulance without the two men who sustained him through CPR. How long ago had God put all of this in motion so he could take care of us that frightening afternoon?

Now I know that no matter what happens, God will take care of me—whether I'm married to my husband or left a widow. I have decided that no matter what happens, I will rejoice. I'm living day by day and trusting him. Trusting is all I can do. Nothing else works.

A Voyage Ends

Nancy Bayless

We were on the fragile edge of exhaustion as we sailed into the serene anchorage at Gun Cay in the Bahamas. We discussed the pros and cons of stopping or continuing to our destination: Fort Lauderdale, Florida. We decided to stop. This would be our last night of more than seven hundred nights aboard our sturdy little thirty-foot ketch.

Two years aboard a small ship can be a trying experience. But for my husband, Lynn, and me, senior citizens who loved the sea and sailing, it had been a marvelous adventure. We wanted the challenge of long-range cruising, so we sold most everything we owned and managed to get our lives down to a duffel bag each.

When that was accomplished, we flew from our stateside home to England, where we purchased a beautiful, brand-new sailboat. After several months of making upgrades, we stowed our provisions and set sail for Gibraltar.

From there we went to the Balearic Islands of Spain in the Mediterranean Sea. Then we followed Columbus's route across the Atlantic and cruised the West Indies, the Virgin Islands, and the Bahamas.

As we entered this quiet Bahamian harbor, our trip was almost over. We threaded our way around a network of assorted craft anchored in the lee of razor-sharp coral banks. When we found an open space, we watched with tired fascination while our anchor chain snaked its way down through the transparent water to the white sand bottom. Coral heads of rich pinks and subtle yellows formed a broken necklace around our hook.

I felt a warm glow of security, and I thanked God for this refuge. Serenity abounded as the sun shot arrows of radiant color in the sky. The placid sea turned red, mirroring the sunset.

We ate a sandwich, then made a last-minute anchor check before climbing into our bunk. Daylight vanished, and a clear, star-filled evening sky hung like a suspended planetarium over our glass hatch.

Lynn reached over and started to rub my back. "It's been a good trip," he said. "Yes," I agreed. "We are very blessed."

His hand became still and heavy as he drifted off to sleep; then while my lips were still praising the Lord, my eyes closed and oblivion surrounded me.

Several hours later, the alarming moan of a rush of wind penetrated my unconsciousness. With the thunder of an express train, the wind roared through our rigging. Our anchor chain stretched taut, and a horrifying shudder passed from the hull of our boat to my bone-weary body.

I groped my way to the pilot house. Lynn staggered out onto the deck. In a matter of minutes, our clear night had been filled with a monstrous, ceiling-zero storm with gale-force winds. We watched in awe as the windswept sea around us became a cauldron of ferocious, phosphorescent waves.

To avoid other boats dragging into us, we decided it would be safer to head out to sea. I started the engine while Lynn tried, without success, to get our anchor up. I went out to help him with the anchor, hooked on my lifeline, and screamed at God, "Stop this storm, Lord! Don't you know we're almost home?"

A white sheet of rain flew across the ocean and pelted against my skin like stinging bees. My body began shaking with uncontrollable spasms. Lynn motioned for me to go back inside, so I stood by the wheel and watched his feet being lifted off the deck. Waves tossed us about like a bathtub toy. I looked at our compass. It resembled a whirling top.

We'd been cold and wet and scared many times during our two-year cruise. We'd survived nasty, short-lived squalls in the Mediterranean, suffered through tropical depressions across the Atlantic, and survived violent electrical storms in the Caribbean. But this was different. This time we were in a gridlock with no sea room and absolutely no visibility. My mind churned in a terrified frenzy of imagined disasters.

Our wind indicator peaked out at sixty-two knots. Due to the change in the wind's direction, the coral banks were now an enemy across our path. They would tear our boat and our bodies to shreds if our anchor didn't hold.

The other sailboats and the small, coastal freighter that had anchored off our stern were menaces too. I envisioned the freighter, or one of the immense sailboats, dragging down on top of us. And there was no way to tell if we were barreling through the night into some unseen peril because our depth sounder was as unstable as our compass, and we had no radar.

Lynn was hanging on desperately as he watched our anchor chain stretch out one minute and go slack the next. The sounds made by the pounding waves and the taut chain were unreal. It sounded as if the entire bow of our boat was being torn apart.

I pleaded with the Lord to stop the storm while frustrated tears streamed down my cheeks. "We can't handle this, Lord! Stop it! Please stop it right this minute! Why are you letting this happen?"

For the first time since giving my life to Jesus, my faith wavered. I felt as if God was turning his back on us. I knew he had protected us through thousands of miles from England to this very spot on the brink of the Florida Keys. But now he was allowing us to possibly lose our boat and even our lives, only fifty miles from home.

I went back on deck, and the vertigo reared its head. I felt as though my body were drawn backwards and tilted sideways. Suddenly, I thought of Jesus' words to his Father on the Mount of Olives: "Father, if you are willing, please take away this cup of horror from me. But I want your will, not mine" (Luke 22:42 TLB).

Did I really want his will? Something stirred deep within me. I knew I wanted his will at any cost. And I knew he hadn't turned away from me.

I had momentarily lost faith in him, though he assured me in John 14:18, "No, I will not abandon you or leave you as orphans in the storm—I will come to you" (TLB).

Guilt surged over me. I'd had the audacity to demand that God return us safely home when he had been with us every mile of the way the entire two years we had lived at sea.

Now we were completely helpless, totally at his mercy. "Oh Father, forgive me! Please let me feel your presence. Please let me know your will."

I could barely see Lynn through the torrential rain. Waves broke over our bow, and water poured from his orange life jacket, but he hadn't slipped and fallen overboard.

I shivered with cold as my fear gradually lessened and my faith revived. The words of my favorite verses began to flow through my mind, "To him who is able to keep you from falling" (Jude 24 NIV).

All at once the storm ended. Stars winked. The lighthouse rose out of the gloom with stately splendor, and the freighter got underway. We had not dragged. In fact, our anchor was caught on something, and we had to use the force of our engine to power over the top of our anchor and break it loose before we could haul it aboard.

Then we followed in the wake of the freighter. We elected to leave because the crews on some of the boats around us were frazzled, and their anchors had tangled together when they dragged into each other. At sea we could take turns sleeping and feel secure in our isolation.

Lynn was pale with fatigue as he silently came in and calculated our compass course. After he finished, he gave me a big hug. "Are you as tired as I am?" he asked.

"No," I said, "you go first." He smiled with weary contentment and headed for our bunk. The freighter veered off toward Miami, and I set our course up the coast to Fort Lauderdale. I hugged myself with happiness. We were going home!

The glow of the mainland lighted the midnight sky. I'd slept for almost four hours before the storm, and now I felt so wide awake. I let Lynn sleep.

I thought about God's grace and peace and his constant forgiveness. I realized how delicate the line is between belief and disbelief.

I finally understood that he always grants me the privilege of choice. I can choose to turn away from him, or I can choose to try to manipulate him. I can also choose to obey him and trust him and choose only his will for my life. I marveled at his strength during my weakness. I knew that he loved me unconditionally and would continue to protect me if I allowed him to do so.

Dawn crept across the sparkling sea, and sunrise filled my eyes and my heart with golden glory. I smiled at the new day. God's will had been done.

The Answered Prayer

Roy Hanschke

I had always prayed for a chance to share my faith with my neighbors, but it seemed I never had the opportunity, that is, until I heard about Jim. I didn't know Jim well. We'd been neighbors for twenty years but never got beyond the casual "Hello. How's it going?" stage. Now Jim was dying, and I felt that God wanted me to talk to him.

I called Jim's wife to ask if I could visit him, and she told me that Jim wanted to see me. I knew he knew of my religious convictions. *Perhaps,* I reasoned, *he's ready to talk about God.*

As I entered the house, I saw Jim sitting in an upholstered chair across the room. That chair was to be the site of our meetings for the next nine months.

Jim looked quite different from the man I had seen working in his yard only a few short weeks ago. As he greeted me, I noted his pale coloring and shaking hands.

I crossed the room and walked toward him. I could feel my heart beating. *Will Jim be open to what I have to say? He wanted to see me; what's on his mind?*

After a bit of polite chatter, I said, "Jim, I'm really sorry this is happening to you. Have you wondered what lies ahead of you after this life?"

Jim's wife, Lillian, answered for him, "Roy, that's why we asked you to come."

I felt my heart racing with excitement. *Thank you,* I prayed silently.

I took a deep breath and plunged ahead. "Jim, God desires to know each of us personally."

Jim nodded.

"God loves you and wants a personal relationship with you to assure you of an eternal place in heaven."

As I continued, I was exhilarated at Jim's rapt attention and keen interest. Finally, I asked, "That's why Christ died and rose again, as payment for our sins. Are you ready to invite Christ into your life to forgive you of your sins so you can know God?"

I paused, waiting for his answer. He blinked. His expression told me he hadn't comprehended anything I had said. *Hadn't I been clear?*

I wildly searched my mind for help, dragging up every illustration I could think of to help clarify my message. Yet each attempt of explaining God's love only produced more confusion. Finally, from behind his chair, I read Lillian's lips, "It's the medication."

I understood. The heavy doses of morphine that eased Jim's pain also fogged his mind, preventing him from being able to comprehend. In frustration and desperation I cried out in my heart, *Oh God, help me!*

I don't remember what I said next. After a few moments I prayed for Jim and excused myself, promising to visit him again soon. Jim's smile returned to his face just as I had seen it when I first entered his home.

What's happening? What are you showing me, God?

I returned to see Jim a week later. Once again we exchanged pleasantries. "Jim, how are you feeling?"

He answered weakly, "I have my good days and bad. Today I'm in a lot of pain. But I'm glad you came."

My mind was racing. *Why am I here? What made Jim glad to see me? What do I have to offer him that he can understand?*

I've forgotten most of what we said that second visit, but before I left, I took Jim's hands and prayed for him. "Lord, give Jim peace, strength, and comfort."

When I opened my eyes, his were filled with tears. "Thanks," he said and then added, "Would you teach me how to pray like you pray?"

Teach Jim to pray? If that's what Jim wants, why not? I wasn't sure what else to do.

It wasn't until later that the significance of his request hit me. Jim didn't want to talk *about* God. He wanted to talk *to* God. After all, he didn't have much time. They had told him he had less than a year. I had been trying to explain what a relationship with God was all about, but Jim just wanted to start one.

"Teach me how to pray like you pray," meant, "help me cry out to God."

With renewed enthusiasm I asked God to help me somehow feel what Jim was feeling so that I could help him tell God, in his words, what was on his heart. On my next visit I listened more.

He told me, "I'm so concerned about my wife; what will happen to her when I'm gone?" He talked about his daughter and son-in-law. He spoke of a brother back east who needed God in his life. He revealed his own fears.

Over the next eight months, Jim and I met often. Each time I brought a hand-written prayer that I had penned, written from Jim's perspective. Every time I entered his house I'd notice him looking at my hands to see my paper prayers. He was like a child anticipating a special treat. His eyes would light up, and he would smile when he spotted the sheet of paper I held. Together we would pray the words on that page. Sometimes we'd pray them more than once.

In spite of his pain, Jim would wait until after I left to take his medication so that his mind would be as clear as possible while I was there. Leaning forward, he would take my hand, and together we would pour out our hearts to God.

"Lord, I hear you knocking on the door of my life. The door is open. Please come in."

"Dear God, my heart gets troubled and I fear the unknown. Help me bring every anxiety to you in exchange for your peace."

"Lord, it's hard not to worry. I worry about the people I love. I worry about the future. I worry about myself. Guard my heart and mind as I live each day and each moment with you and for you."

"Lord, I want to do what is right, but I suffer so much and feel like a burden to others. I want you to take me home. I know there's another side to my suffering. With my faith in you, I am able to encourage those around me. So I will leave my life in your hands. As long as you keep me here, let me know you better and serve you more. Keep me strong until my work for you is done. Amen."

Then came that beautiful June morning. It was already warm, but the breeze was gentle and cool. As the birds rehearsed their hopeful song, we prayed once again. "For thine is the kingdom and the power and the glory forever. Amen."

The voices gave way to silence. Every hand held the hand of someone nearby, every hand except Jim's. His were gently folded, resting peacefully inside a casket at the head of which my hand rested.

The family had asked me to preside at the service. "What do you want me to say?" I inquired of them.

"Share what you and Dad shared for the past nine months," was the reply.

The day of the funeral, as I stood before Jim's friends and family, I realized that half the people there were our neighbors. As I read each expression that Jim and I had shared with God, I gratefully recalled the simple prayer I had prayed before all of this happened. "God let me share my faith in you with my neighbors."

For Jim's sake, as well as my own, I am grateful God answered.

Today I can still picture Jim in his upholstered chair, his ready smile on his face. Only now I know he's finally free of pain. And I know Jim no longer needs my paper prayers, for he can speak with God face to face. For you see, death was not a period at the end of Jim's life, but merely a comma. I know that someday Jim and I will meet again. And who knows, maybe we'll even be neighbors.

All Is Calm, All Is Bright

Marlene Bagnull

"Ninety and still going strong."

This was an apt description of my remarkable Aunt Laura. Although she was arthritic, almost blind in one eye, and hard of hearing, she still managed, by choice, to live by herself in a second-floor apartment.

Laura wasn't really alone. She had her cat, a beautiful part Persian we had given her as a kitten. What a proud and handsome fellow he was! He would sit grooming his bushy tail for hours and then climb into Laura's lap purring. How she loved him and spoiled him. He filled those long, lonely hours when Laura wasn't off somewhere doing something.

She often visited family and friends, even traveling across the continent the summer she turned ninety. She also taught the two- and three-year-olds in Sunday school until she was ninety. She loved those youngsters, and they loved her.

Laura never had any children of her own, so she adopted other people's children, including ours. Laura, you see, was not really my aunt. By mutual agreement we had chosen to become family, much to the delight of my three children.

The year Laura turned ninety-two was a hard one for her. She knew she was slowing down. Often she choked back tears and told me how she feared, not death, but having to go into a nursing home. She was afraid she'd be forgotten and no longer needed. I assured her we would always need her.

One special day the church organist called Laura to tell her the choir needed her. You see, Laura had been a paid soloist in her younger days. Her voice still revealed her years of training. She beamed when she told me she had been asked to sing, and she faithfully began to go to every rehearsal, even when she didn't feel up to it.

I often worried that Laura was trying to do too much; yet I had to admire her. She was an inspiration to everyone who met her. Knowing her somehow made all of us have fewer fears about growing old.

Early one morning Laura's neighbor called to say that Laura had just been taken to the hospital. "It looks like a stroke," she said.

I threw on my clothes and got to the hospital as fast as I could. Laura was lying on a cot in the emergency room. She was white-faced, and her hands were cold. The corner of her mouth drooped as she tried to form words. "My cat, he'll starve."

"Don't worry, we'll take care of him," we tried to comfort her.

As the morning progressed, Laura began to speak better. It was a transitory stroke, the doctors said. She would recover. And she seemed to be doing so before my very eyes. Yet that evening when I returned to the hospital, I was distressed to discover she was worse. It was impossible for me to make out more than a few words.

Laura's eyes filled with frustration and tears as she slumped back on the pillows. I smoothed back some stray wisps of hair and sought to comfort her. She clung to me and wept.

The next few days Laura grew weaker. Family and friends came in and out discussing her "condition." I tried to shush them. I knew she heard and understood everything they were saying, even though she couldn't respond.

One night after visiting hours had ended, I snatched a few extra moments alone with Laura. I took both of her hands in mine and reminded her how she had always been an inspiration to everybody.

"You can't let them see you giving up," I told her. "And you can't listen to everything they say. Where's your spunk and strong will? If anyone can recover, you can."

Laura tried to speak but then shook her head in exasperation.

"You will talk and walk again," I encouraged her. "You'll surprise them all. How about if I pray for you?"

Laura nodded her head. God's presence filled the room as I began to pray for strength and healing. When I left that evening, I knew he had touched her.

I visited Laura every night and prayed for her. After days of no improvement, however, my faith began to erode. Driving home one cold night, I gave in to the despair I was feeling. The holidays were coming, but I told the Lord I just couldn't get into the Christmas spirit. Problems at home were pressing down on me. I was tired and depressed and so very worried about Laura.

"We're giving a concert at the hospital," the church organist called the next day to tell me. "Do you think you can get permission to bring Laura?"

"I'm sure I can. She will love it," I replied.

Laura was sitting in her wheelchair waiting for me the night of the concert. Her eyes sparkled as I pushed her into the hospital cafeteria. She was like a little child as she pointed to the tree and clapped her hands.

While we waited, Laura struggled to express her questions. Were members of her church choir really going to be there? And the director?

Her speech was still very hard to understand, but it was getting better. God was answering my prayers, yet that familiar heaviness descended as I thought of the future she faced. She would never be able to return to her home and take care of herself or her cat.

The cat. I shuddered as I thought of it. Despite my protests, her nephew had done what I knew was the only realistic and sensible thing. He had taken it to the animal shelter. None of us had the courage to tell Laura.

"You're my best friend—my pal," Laura said, interrupting my thoughts. She squeezed my hand with the one that hadn't been working a week ago.

The concert began. Sometimes Laura leaned forward in excitement, and other times she relaxed back into the wheelchair and closed her eyes. She had a beautiful smile on her face as the time passed all too quickly.

"OK, let's lower the lights and sing just one more carol," the director said. Motioning to the audience of patients, staff, and friends, he invited us to sing along.

"Silent night! Holy night!" we began to sing. I turned my head in amazement. Laura was singing clearly, without hesitation, "All is calm, all is bright."

I knew I was witnessing a miracle. Not only was Laura singing like she had before her stroke; her face reflected the peace and hope of the words she sang.

As I listened and joined my voice with hers, my heaviness of heart suddenly lifted. All within me felt calm and bright. I rejoiced anew in the birth of Christ my Savior. Just as he had been with Laura, he would also be with me. His love and his grace would see us both through the heartache and pain that is sometimes part of our lives here on earth, and one glorious day we would both meet him face to face.

4
Love Lets Go

I bend, but I do not break.
Jean de la Fontaine

Chimborazo, 1863

Steve Wise

On a cold winter night in 1863, a life and death drama was played out within the walls of Chimborazo Hospital in Richmond, Virginia. Of all the thousands of poignant memories that have been passed down from those who lived through the Civil War, this one, for me, stands alone. It is the story of two people, linked forever in blood and horror and yet bound on a higher plane far beyond the travails of earth. I read their story on a cold winter night in Missouri, 130 years after the anguish was lived out, but the moan of the wind around the corner of my house sounded very old. Perhaps it was the same wind they heard that night. Listen with me to the old wind as we listen with them.

Phoebe Pember had grown to love the boy named Fisher. Wounded in battle months before, he somehow escaped the surgeon's knife and saw. The leg would heal now, or so everyone thought, and Phoebe delighted in watching him hobble between the long rows of cots as he attempted to rebuild strength in muscles long dormant. His smile was unfailing, his demeanor simply marvelous, especially for one so young. He had never complained, not once that the nurse could remember, despite the pain and deprivation that was endemic to a Confederate hospital late in the war.

Then came the fateful night. Shortly after one of Fisher's nightly walks, he cried out for help from his cot. Phoebe rushed to his side and saw great spurts of blood pumping from his wound. Deep within his thigh, a bone fragment had loosened and cut into an artery. She quickly pressed her fingers over the wound and stemmed the bright red flow. The nurse called for the surgeon on duty, and after a brief examination, he spoke in muffled tones to Phoebe. The artery was too deeply encased in the fleshy part of the leg, he informed her, and then walked away. The boy was doomed.

"Long I sat by the boy," she later wrote, "holding fast against the open artery, once a wonderful vessel that carried the substance of life, and now, a hidden agent of death."

After long minutes of silence, she could no longer withhold the surgeon's diagnosis. Quietly, and with all the calm she could muster, Phoebe Pember pronounced the death sentence. The boy took the news with great equanimity, even peace. He told her exactly what he wanted to be written to his mother; he made his pitiful arrangements. Then he looked into Phoebe's eyes.

"How long can I live?"

"Only as long as I keep my fingers on this artery."

Fisher fell silent, and the woman wondered what could be passing through his mind, this child who would never again see his mother busy in her kitchen, who would never again feel the sturdy clasp of his father's hand on his shoulder. After a long pause, he calmly spoke again.

"You can let go now."

But Phoebe could not. "No more than if my own life trembled in the balance," she later said. Deep into the winter night, the hushed tragedy unfolded—the woman, softly weeping, a study in grim resolve. Her own blood pounded in her ears, her lips went cold, yet she held fast, shifting from one agonizing position to another.

Then something very strange happened. It was as if God looked down on the two forlorn figures, huddled together in their hopeless struggle, and said, "Take your rest, dear woman; he belongs to me now." For the only time in three years of nearly continuous mental and physical anguish, a time of little or no rest and meager rations, a time when thousands of pleading moans and cries came to her ears like tiny daggers—amid the incredible sum of it all—for the first and only time in her life, Phoebe Pember fainted. She regained consciousness only to find that her clothing was soaked with the dead boy's blood. The nurse willed her trembling legs to allow her to stand, and then she began to prepare Fisher's body for burial.

I do not claim to know the destination of the fallen soldier's soul when, in that transcendent moment that awaits us all, he crossed the great divide. But, certainly, the essence of Christianity fairly exuded from his last acts on earth. Even the boy's final words paralleled those of Christ when, in his fleeting moments on the cross, he said, "Father, into your hands I commend my spirit."

It is only with the knowledge that comes from a union with Jesus Christ that we may, in our turn, pronounce our own benedictions to whomever holds fast to our death wounds. May we say it with the boy.

"You can let go now."

Gramma Jan

Jan Coleman

When I drove into the park, I recognized Grace right away, sitting quietly on a bench watching children romp and play. *Why did she have to come?* I thought. *Couldn't she let me be "Gramma" for the day? I've waited so long.*

When I walked up, Grace looked at me tenderly. "I've thought about you so much these last few years." She was constantly in my mind too—the woman who was grandmother to my daughter's child.

My mind went back six years, when Amy, seventeen, told me she was pregnant. I had struggled solo after Amy's dad left us seven years before and thought the worst was behind us, until that day. On her own, Amy decided to place the baby for adoption. It was the right thing for this confused, young girl, and I was touched that she asked me to help her choose the parents through an open adoption process. I was fine until I saw the ultrasound, the life growing inside my daughter. Then it hit me. In a few months I, too, would have to let go and say good-bye to the baby.

Leslie, the adoptive mom, assured me, "We want you to be a part of her life."

What role could I possibly have? Leslie's mother, Grace, had waited sixty-three years to spoil a grandchild. How much would she want me around?

After little Nicole was born, Amy brought her home for a week. "I need time to say good-bye."

Those were special days—days to make memories

with her first child, to hold her, sing to her, write her a loving letter, and then to let her go. Yet I couldn't get close, scared that embracing this child would only increase my sorrow when she left us.

The first time I met Grace was when she came to my house to see her new infant granddaughter. "I know you'll love her very much," I said stiffly, biting my lip. Thankfully, Grace said nothing but merely hugged me.

After everyone left, Amy couldn't stop crying. Trying to shore up my daughter's courage, I took her straight to the Bible, to First Samuel. We talked about Samuel, how his mother had first given him to the Lord and then to the prophet Eli to raise her much-longed-for son. "It wasn't easy for Hannah to give him up to be raised by someone else," I said. "Little did Hannah know that her son would be a prophet of the Lord. We read on, 'Those who honor me I will honor.' Hannah was blessed with more children to take the place of the one she prayed for."

Amy took it to heart. Her faith grew, and God used her as an instrument in his repair work in the lives of other unmarried pregnant girls. Each time she shared her story, Amy grew more confident of God's leading in her life.

I got to see Nikki crawl and start to walk, but after her first birthday, her adoptive dad, Keith, was transferred to Florida. Leslie promised many pictures and videos, but I was bonded with the baby now. How will she ever know me, living three thousand miles away? I felt cheated.

The years went by, and with every photo I ached. Nikki was the image of my daughter! I swallowed my hurt in a secret part of my heart.

The family was making their first trip back to California, and they asked me to meet them at the park. Driving down the freeway, I selfishly hoped Grace wouldn't be there. I wanted Nikki to myself just for a few hours, but I was fearful. *How will she respond to a woman she doesn't know?* I thought.

"She knows she's adopted," Leslie told me on the phone. "We're not sure how much she understands, but you are her Gramma Jan."

What a delightful, loving child I met that day. We played hide and seek and fed the ducks. She sat on my lap while I fixed her ponytail, and Grace sat quietly in the background. I was ashamed of my attitude toward this woman who lived up to her beautiful name. At the end of the day, Grace nudged me aside. "You've done better than I thought you would, Jan. I know how hard this must be for you."

The tears stung. "Oh, Grace, this is making me cry."

"She's a special child, Jan. She's such a blessing to me."

It was easy to see. Nikki was secure, adored by her father, and thrilled with two little brothers.

"Please come and see us in Florida when you can," Keith said, hugging me good-bye. It was as if God reached down with comforting arms to say, *This day was my gift to you, Jan. You will have a place in her life.*

As Grace said her good-byes to me, she glanced over at Nikki, who was feeding the squirrels. "Thank you," she said, squeezing my hand.

She was thanking me because Nikki was her gift from God, a gift that came through me! I had missed the joy because I held on so firmly to my loss, some-how blaming God for not giving me another baby girl to grandmother. But, there is only one Nikki, and God has a special plan for her life. He chose me to play a special part in it, and that's where my joy must come from.

That day in the park, I finally let go. As I glanced back at Nikki chasing another squirrel, I put my arms around Grace. "Thank *you* for having room in your heart to let me be 'Gramma Jan.'"

Letting Go

Betsy Dill

The house echoes. . . .

It's shiny and clean and featureless—a museum to the past. It echoes a thousand hours of laughter and loud music, frantic last-minute trips and rustling bags of junk food. It is silent, like a stilled voice after an argument—the breathless pondering that follows a great truth expressed and digested. It is my home, but it is halved, hushed, and emptied of the vitality of a son grown past a messy bedroom and a midnight raid on the fridge. It is predictable and sane. Things remain where I leave them. I can find everything—except my son and my heart.

I pass a mirror and stare at my reflection for the first time in years. How long has it been since I really looked at myself? When did my eyes grow old? It must have happened when I changed his diapers. Or maybe when I taught him to ride a bike, then drive a car, or endlessly nagged him about taking out the trash. Countless nights sleeping with one eye open, waiting for the familiar sound of a key in the lock and his tread upon the steps.

I stand in the doorway looking back over my shoulder, reluctant to let go. It was difficult, sometimes frustrating, but profoundly worthwhile and exhilarating, this child rearing. Will anything ever be this rewarding again in life? What compares to creating life? What to that of raising a child? I don't want to go back as much as I want to hold on to today for just a little longer. Then I will leap into new creative pursuits, and I will smile at these memories. Today, however, the house echoes, and I whisper, "Good-bye, son of my heart. I will miss you."

"Good-bye, My Baby"

Nancy Kennedy

I wave good-bye and watch her cross the street to school. There's a big test today. *How big can a test be in the fourth grade?* I wonder.

Skipping up the hill in her dirty high-top sneakers, wearing a neon orange T-shirt over black stretch pants and a neon yellow baseball cap positioned just so, she knows she looks cool. She is cool, even with several teeth missing and a drop of maple syrup on her chin.

"Watch out for cars!" I shout from across the street. I want to go with her, to hold her hand, to shield her from heartache, sorrow, tough spelling words, and bee stings.

"Mom, I'm almost nine and a half," I've been told. "I can cross the street alone."

I follow her to the corner anyway, "just to mail a letter." I wave good-bye to my baby. In her place, a fourth grader who's almost nine and a half waves back.

When I return home, my oldest daughter sits in the driver's seat of my car, impatiently pushing radio buttons. "Let me back the car out," she pleads.

I shudder at the sight of her behind the wheel. *Will she really be driving soon?*

"Move over," I laugh, despite the tears welling in my eyes. I don't want my baby driving. I'm not ready.

As we near the high school, she instructs me, "Let me out here."

Is it me she doesn't want to be seen with? Is it the

group of girls standing in front of the school who scare her?

"How do they get the front of their hair to stick out like that?" I ask.

She rolls her eyes at me and sighs, "Oh, Mom."

"Do you have lunch money?" I ask. "Are your gym clothes clean?"

She rolls her eyes again.

I stifle the urge to brush a strand of hair from her cheek. Someone might see. Instead, I wave good-bye to my baby who's now two inches taller than I am. She's wearing *my* jeans, *my* pink cashmere sweater, and *my* silver hoop earrings.

Wasn't it yesterday that I dressed her in ruffled sunsuits and white eyelet bonnets?

Where did the time go? How can it be that never again will she sit on my lap and play "I've got your nose"? I'm not even sure where I fit in her life anymore. She's almost a woman—she *is* a woman. And I'm acutely aware of her soft curves and mane of brown curls that draw admiring glances from young men.

She's making plans for college in two years. She dreams of a life apart from me—a career, a husband, a baby. My baby with a baby?

Later that night I tuck my youngest daughter into bed. She says, "In Sunday school we learned that God is way bigger than the sky and that he never sleeps." She turns over and yawns a sleepy, "I'm glad."

"Me too," I whisper.

The next day I go to the market and see a pair of brown eyes peeking out from under a mop of brown curls. They belong to a little girl standing in the checkout line in front of me. I smile, thinking how much she looks like my long-ago babies.

She has a silver balloon tied to her wrist, and I watch her struggle to untie it. Her mother watches, too, fretting and scolding. "Hold on tight," she says. "Don't let go."

The little girl keeps struggling with the string. I watch the way the balloon bobs and weaves while it is still tied at her wrist. It wants to fly.

Following her out of the store, I notice she's still struggling with her balloon. As I watch them get into their car and drive away, I wonder what would've happened if she had let it go.

I pause at my car and look up at the clouds. "God's way bigger than the sky," I say to myself.

I think about how I've tried to keep my daughters tied to my wrist and how they've struggled with the string. They want to fly. They need to fly. I need to let them. I need to let God hold their strings, and trust that his grasp is infinitely stronger than mine.

I run back into the store and buy two silver balloons. When I return to my car, I look again into the sky. I hesitate. I can feel my stomach knotting.

It's hard to let go.

I slowly release my grip on the balloons, sending them heavenward.

I watch them dip and dance as they soar to heights they could never achieve if tied to my wrist. I watch for a long time, smiling and at peace.

Pat's Hands

Mimi Deeths

Pat was a darling little blonde with spirit and a smile. I liked her immediately. She, like me, had been diagnosed with colon cancer, and we were receiving our chemotherapy in the same office. Comparing experiences and griping about the undesirable side effects of the medication brought about an automatic sense of camaraderie. Misery loves company, and that was obvious from the laughter that flowed from both of us on that first day we met.

I confessed to Pat that I worked out some of my frustration by writing a book about my experiences, but I mentioned casually that most of my book was still inside my head because I was such a poor typist. Pat laughed and said, "We make a great pair. I am an executive secretary, and I love to type, but I have no ideas for a book of my own. Why don't you tell me your story, and I will type it."

So we started to get together, and I poured out my feelings about my disease as Pat listened. Mine was a story of faith through the experience of a life-threatening disease. Pat was interested, then over-whelmed. She said she admired the faith I possessed in the face of adversity and encouraged me to share more of it with her. Over the next year and a half, Pat learned more about the God whom she had placed behind other priorities in her life.

She felt that God was angry with her and did not pay attention to her. I assured her that if she began to pray, God would hear her prayers. She returned to church after many years away, and her family began to accompany her there. They became united under the embrace of God's love, and Pat chose to let God take control of her life.

Pat's cancer is spreading. She will not recover, but she now knows how to approach the throne of God.

It is hard to say good-bye to the special friend I have known for too short a time. I have to do the typing myself now, but I'm getting better at it. Yesterday I carefully typed this note to Pat to let her know I have relieved her of her typing duties. She's in hospice care now, and I think she's about to be promoted from secretary to saint.

To my dear friend, Pat —
What do you do when the agony is too much to bear?
Seek God's face and learn to love him more.
He asks no longer that you be his hands reaching out on
    this earth to do his work.

He invites you now to rest your hands—
those hands that prayed and sought his work to do,
those little girl's hands with which you once discovered
    the world around you,
the tender arms that held babies and directed little
    children in the right way to live,
the working hands that kept a tidy house,
the fast flying fingers that typed so efficiently,
the loving hands that provided a ready reach for those in
    need,

the tiny delicate hands that slip gently into the strong
   hands of the man you love,
the weary hands that reach out and say to loved ones,
   "I need you near."

Lay your hands to rest now, Pat . . .
   and seek the face of God.
He loves you and you will see the love in his eyes.
You are his precious child.
He wants to take you to his heart, brave warrior.
Your battle is over.

                    Love,
                    Mimi

Editor's Note: Pat has now graduated to saint. Mimi was privileged to share this letter of good-bye at Pat's funeral. We know these two will meet again in God's time. What a day that will be!

Toward the End of the Journey

Charlotte Adelsperger

Nothing could have kept me from going to be with my twin sister Alberta and her family on that Friday afternoon in early April 1976. Alberta and Ron Heil's thirteen-year-old son Mark had been fighting leukemia for seven years. Now Mark was no longer in remission. Medical reports showed he was sliding rapidly downhill. As my bus sped across Missouri and headed for Saint Louis, I shivered from stirrings of apprehension. Alberta's latest call indicated the disease was out of control. *How would Mark be? How would his family be coping?*

When Alberta met my bus, that special love and closeness we know as twins bounded into full force. I knew immediately when I saw her that the burden was heavy. We hugged. As soon as we got in the car, she began to cry softly, and I wrapped my arms around her.

"Mark had a checkup today," she said. "After the doctor saw the reports, he talked with me alone, and he called Ron. There is nothing more medical science can do." Her voice broke. "He said Mark could die anytime—even in the next three days."

I was stunned.

As we drove to the house, Alberta shared her reaction to the heartbreaking news. She and Ron lived in utter dependence on God and viewed the doctors as a means through which God works, but even now they were not giving up hope.

I breathed a prayer as I entered Mark's room. There I found him resting in bed and watching TV with his little sister Diana who, as usual, was lifting his spirits. When he saw me, a broad smile danced across the pallor of his face. We chatted. Oh, the sweetness of his spirit! And such a calm maturity for a boy about to turn fourteen.

Waves of memories flooded my mind. I recalled when Mark was interviewed on the radio by his "Pastor Ken" just a few months before. I knew Mark's message by heart, having listened often to the taped broadcast. Mark told the listening audience, "Jesus really came into my life about a year ago. I've known about Jesus ever since I was a little kid, but I finally accepted him as my Lord and Savior. We can't live without him and be happy."*

Mark interrupted my thoughts with questions about what was going on in my life. As always, he had a way of making people feel special. That was his "love style."

Alberta, Ron, and Diana moved with amazing naturalness that evening. One might have expected emotional chaos to spring up at any point. But it didn't. Instead, I saw serenity in Ron and Alberta—a steadfastness. The kind God gives. Privately they talked with me, sharing their grief. Yet there was no panic, no self-pity. They were living one moment at a time.

Beautiful love for one another was the hallmark of their home. And we all savored just being with Mark. That night I started a sketchy journal about my visit. I wrote, "The peace and presence of God is very real in this house. What a comfort!"

What were the ingredients for such a remarkable climate at this time of crisis? Alberta had shared in a letter: "Each one of us has come to know the love and power of the Lord in a deeper way. But we have hardly 'arrived' in our growth. Jesus has arrived on the scene. We invited him a long time ago. We must keep looking to him."

Now, during my visit, I was wondering what God was doing. The morning after my arrival, there was a noticeable change in Mark. He was rallying! His pain was under control. He ate pancakes, walked around, and we played a game at the table.

"Mark, you're having a good day," I commented.

"You revived me," he returned with a warm smile. I was touched, but I knew God was answering all the prayers being offered.

Miraculously, Mark gained strength each day. One night his Grandmother and Grandfather Rist took us all out to dinner. Mark moved slowly, but he was able to partake and enjoy. He further amazed us by going to church and Sunday school the next day. God's faithfulness was showing!

On the last morning of my visit, Mark got ready to go to school for a few hours—another miracle. Ron asked the four of us to gather with him in a prayer circle to thank God for my visit. I was holding Mark's hand, and praying silently that I wouldn't break into tears. My throat tightened as we kissed good-bye. "I love you, Mark," I whispered.

He climbed into the car with his father while I stood on the porch, a forced smile quivering on my face. I waved. I waved again. I knew he couldn't hear me weep as they slowly drove away. Mark sat so tall and straight, his blonde wig covering his baldness from chemotherapy. The car turned, and I could no longer see them. "O God," I prayed, "hold him close— no matter what happens—hold him close!" I was surely echoing the prayers of all who loved him.

Two weeks later Mark's courageous journey drew to a close during Holy Week. On Maundy Thursday evening he received his last solid food, Holy Communion, lovingly brought by elders of the church. On Good Friday morning, Mark's nose began to bleed. It wouldn't stop. By nightfall he was in the hospital.

Alberta shared glimpses of those last hours:

Ron and I were numb as we kept the all-night vigil with Mark. We gave him drinks, held his hand, and expressed our love.

"Mark, I love everything about you," I said. He smiled.

On Saturday morning, April 17, Mark's breathing became rapid, but he was alert.

"Something good has got to come out of this," he said.

"Yes, Mark," I replied, "God works all things together for good." He began to breathe faster. I was praying to God in the depths of my being, crying, *Help! Help Mark.*

Ron kept his hand on Mark's shoulder. "God is with you, Mark," he repeated over and over in his strong, loving tone. Our pastor slipped into the room.

Silence. Utter stillness—except for Mark's breathing.

Then Mark gazed past all of us, looking straight ahead: "I see Jesus!"

Instantly we began hugging him, all of us thanking God at once. Victory was in the air, but I wasn't sure what was happening. Mark's eyes were shining. Tears were streaming down my face. I cried, "Thank you, Lord, thank you!"

Within thirty minutes our son died. In distant parts of the world, Easter morning was already breaking forth with all of Christ's promises of eternal life. But Mark Heil was personally receiving the fulfillment of those promises—to live "ever with the Lord."

Footnote: These are the exact words of Mark Heil taken from the tape of the 1976 radio broadcast. Mark Ronald Heil (1962–76) lived in Kirkwood, Missouri.

Death's Colors

Dayle Allen Shockley

On a sultry day in summer, I watch my husband trudge up the steps of our home, looking grim. The past few weeks have been draining. His father, Ernest, has undergone a battery of tests after a routine checkup on his lungs. Hoping for the best, we fear for the worst.

I tense as Stan opens the front door, letting in a rush of oppressive Texas heat.

"Well? What did they say?" I ask, trying to sound cheerful. He draws his breath in sharply. "It doesn't look good."

Silence hangs between us like a black blanket.

"Daddy has between three months and two years to live—lung cancer."

Ernest is fifty-nine.

Without speaking, Stan and I reach out to each other, our hearts one giant ache.

For several weeks I manage to keep my spirits up. Ernest looks good. He eats well. He still drives Mildred around town. I find myself thinking that this handsome, robust man cannot possibly be terminally ill.

Prayers are offered for Ernest. We wait for a miracle. But by the first signs of autumn, Ernest's condition worsens. The days grow shorter, the nights cooler. Despite this pleasant change, my grief is never far away.

Later one evening, I sit alone in my living room, a rosy piece of sun streaming through the curtains.

94

Outside, an occasional breeze blows from the north, ruffling the tip-top of the large tree in the front yard.

Until that moment I had not noticed that the leaves' colors have changed from summer green to dazzling gold. (It's funny how we often miss beautiful things when we are focused on our problems.)

As I stare out the window, each gust of wind sends a shower of yellow leaves to the ground below. A lovely sight, it is. Yet, I am somewhat startled at the realization that the glorious colors of autumn are actually nature's colors of death. This gives me a peculiar feeling. *Soon the tree will be barren*—I think—*stripped, until its rebirth in the spring.*

At once my thoughts turn to Ernest. *Is his death sentence somehow related to the lovely golden leaves before me?* I wonder.

Some hidden force propels me out the front door. Frantically, I scoop a clump of leaves in my hands and fling them high above my head. I long to put them back on the tree, demand that they stay there. But I can't.

My chest pounding, I lean back against the tree's trunk, a patch of sun falling across my lap. I put my head in my hands and weep.

In mid-October, Ernest and Mildred drive across town to spend a few days with us. Even though Ernest looks tired and frail, his spirits seem high.

After supper one evening, I find Ernest propped upright on the sofa, the lamp glowing against his head, his cheeks pale. Mildred sits at the piano, her fingers playing the keys. It is a late-night kind of tune, slow and easy, and the sight of them there in the yellow light brings a sigh to my lips.

Soon Ernest captures the melody. Faintly at first, his rich baritone voice swells, rising and falling to the music, filling the room, sending a shiver up my spine.

In years past Ernest sang professionally, traveling around with gospel quartets; Mildred, an accompanist. Some kind of sight they must have been.

The last note fades; I applaud softly. "PaPaw," I call to him, "do you want to go and lie down now?"

He smiles. "Hey, this feels good right here. Come on in and join us."

I do, and for the next couple of hours he entertains me with stories about the growing-up years of his four children. Even though I've heard each one—down to the tiniest detail—dozens of times before, this night the stories take on new dimensions. They are funnier. Richer. Sweeter. I know that Ernest is telling them for the last time.

In November, Ernest is admitted to the hospital. A few days later he suffers a stroke that paralyzes a portion of his face. He cannot speak; he utters strange noises.

Through persistence—and patience—we learn to differentiate between the low rumbling tones he makes. He smiles, a victorious smile.

A week before Thanksgiving, the doctor tells us it won't be long now. For hours I watch Ernest's children taking turns sitting by the bed of their father, clutching his ashen hand, smoothing back his damp hair. They sing to him; feebly, he sings to them. They whisper, "We love you, Daddy." He nods knowingly. And Mildred is always there.

We schedule round-the-clock vigils. The nights are exhausting. We drink pots of coffee, staring out into the night, wishing, wondering, hoping.

A week later, Ernest draws his final breath, his family huddled around him. With no struggle, he closes his eyes and sleeps, yielding himself into the arms of his Lord.

The day after the funeral, I come home and walk to the towering tree on the front yard. One golden leaf is all that remains.

Reaching up, I touch the leaf, setting it free. As I do, the little leaf speaks to me about life and death. It says: *Life is but a season. Temporary. Fleeting. Death will surely come. But be encouraged! For with death comes a promise—the promise of spring. The advent of a new life.*

Suddenly I feel a burst of strength. My sorrow becomes bearable. For there is yet another life to come . . . one that will never know the colors of death.

5
Love Laughs

Cheerfulness is the atmosphere
in which all things thrive.
Jean Paul Righter

Surprise for Grandpa

Doris Smalling

My husband and I agreed that a new cereal we bought did not meet our taste expectations. But we disliked the idea of throwing it out.

"I wonder if Heather would eat it?" he asked.

"She'd probably eat it all if you told her it was your new special cereal," I laughed. Our five-year-old granddaughter loved teasing her grandfather when she stayed with us. She always laughed when she "ate Grandpa's cereal all gone."

The following weekend, Grandpa showed her his "new" cereal. Each morning Heather ate a hefty bowl. Just before returning home Monday morning, she emptied the remainder into a plastic sandwich bag and hid it under her jacket. She pointed to her grandpa, who was reading his paper, and winked.

Several weeks later she visited again. As she burst through the door, she ran to her grandpa with a wrapped gift.

"Surprise for you, Grandpa."

Grandpa removed the wrapping and stared at the gift.

Heather kissed him happily. "I'm sorry I ate your new cereal, Grandpa. I saved my allowance all this time and bought you a new box."

Just a Pinch of Salt

Bonnie Compton Hanson

That glorious cake Mother baked for my eighth birth-day—a yellow cake positively slathered in frosting—decided it for me. I wanted to bake a cake too.

You see, my mother was the best cook in the entire world, especially when it came to making her to-die-for cakes. At ten, my older sister Betty was already following in her footsteps. Surely it couldn't be that hard! So that's what I wished for when I blew out my candles and even when I opened my presents.

"Well, Bonnie," Daddy asked, "did you get every-thing you wanted for your birthday?"

"Everything except another cake."

My whole family stared at me. "My goodness!" Mother exclaimed. "Didn't you like the one I baked for you?"

I ran over and threw my arms around her. "Oh, Mother!" I cried. "You know you bake the best cakes in the whole world. I just want to learn how to do it too!"

Mom laughed. "Well, dear, I used all my baking supplies up on your birthday cake. But when we go to the store Saturday, we'll get what you need for your cake."

I could hardly wait for Saturday to come! When my parents came home from shopping, I helped set all those wonderful ingredients out on the counter: vanilla, flour, eggs, two kinds of sugar, baking powder, butter, and even a box of salt.

Later that afternoon Mother brought out a large, well-thumbed cookbook. "Now, Bonnie, this is the recipe we'll use for your very first cake. It's simple but delicious. Put the flour in this mixing bowl after you sift it."

"Sift it? What does that mean?"

Well, I found out right away. Then came the baking powder, sugar, butter, eggs, and all the rest. It was hard to believe this liquidy goo would soon be a gorgeous cake I'd made all by myself!

Finally it was ready to pour into the cake pan. "Now we have to wait twenty-five minutes," Mother said as she turned on a little timer. "So I'm going down to the basement to start on my laundry."

I waited eagerly by the oven door. The wonderful smells that soon drifted out made me positively drool. Finally the timer rang. "It's ready!" I shouted.

Mother hurried back upstairs. Opening the oven door, she carefully lifted out the pan. "Beautiful, Bonnie! I couldn't have done better myself!"

"Can we frost it yet?"

"No, it has to cool a while first, dear. I'll set it by an open window with the timer back on. Call me again when it rings."

By now I felt I had waited all day! But the timer finally rang again. Just as we were finishing the frosting, the washing machine began making wild, clanging noises.

"Oh, dear!" Mother cried, dashing for the basement stairs. "Just add the vanilla and salt," she called back. "Then put the frosting on the cake."

I glanced nervously at the frosting recipe. "It says 'a pinch of salt,' Mother," I yelled downstairs. "What's a pinch of salt?"

"Oh, you know," she shouted back as she battled the washer. "It's just a pinch!"

I carefully measured out the vanilla and poured it in. Then I figured out the "pinch of salt" as best I could and spread the frosting over the cake.

It was gorgeous!

That night after dinner, Mother brought the cake out to show everyone. Daddy smiled from ear to ear. "Look at that! It's beautiful!"

I proudly cut the cake into slices and passed them around. When everyone was served, Daddy said, "Now let's dig in!"

After the first big bite, though, all my brothers and sisters made the strangest faces—and started gulping down water as fast as they could!

"Is something wrong?" I cried.

There was a chorus of "E-excuse me, please!"— and mad dashes to the bathroom. Now only my parents and I were left. Bewildered, I now took a bite of cake too—and spat it right out! It tasted awful!

"But, Mother!" I sobbed. "I followed the recipe exactly. What went wrong?"

Daddy's face was brick-red. He had to gulp down water after every bite. But he kept right on eating. So did Mother. Then, after a big drink, "Bonnie, dear," she answered, "how much salt did you put in the frosting?"

"Oh, like you said—just a pinch. Whatever a *pinch* is. You know, sort of like a handful."

My parents looked at each other. Then they laughed until they cried.

Daddy pulled me to him. "I'm afraid your cake has way too much salt in it, girl," he said. "But the amount of love in it is exactly right!"

And he ate another whole piece!

Loving Enough to Say No

Terry Paulson

I had seen him looking at car magazines, so it was not a complete surprise. After all, when the day for getting your license is in sight, what self-respecting teen is not eagerly dreaming of the car that will give him the freedom he craves? The time was right for a father-son dialogue played out in homes across the United States.

It was a good day, a day Sean hoped to find me in a good mood. When I walked in the front door, he wasted little time. His words hung in the air, "Dad, are you going to get me a car?"

His question was met by my ready answer. "No."

Stunned, he quickly recovered. "Everybody gets a car!" he challenged.

"Sean, I do not think that is true, but even if it were true, it will now be everybody minus one. This will make you a leader! In fact, when you think it through, you will see this will make you popular because you will become the designated rider!

"Since everybody else has a car, they will all want you to ride in their cars. They'll probably fight over you."

His face said it all, *How did I get you for a father?* But instead of voicing his feelings, he moved to plan B. "My birthday is coming up," he prompted. "Will you give me anything toward my car?"

I used a line from Bill Cosby that I had saved for such a moment, "I'll match what your friends will give you."

"That won't be much."

"Bingo! In fact, I think the amount will be well within my budget."

Now in panic, reality was settling in, and Sean was not afraid to share his despair. "Well, how am I going to get a car?"

"I only know three ways. One, you can work hard for someone else, save a big chunk of what you make, and keep saving and working until you have enough money to buy your car. Two, you can start your own company, or three, you can invent something that someone else can sell. Those are the ways you make money."

"I can't start a company!" Sean pleaded.

"Sean, there are teens who are millionaires because they had a dream and the drive to make it happen. In fact, I'd love for one of them to be you."

"But, Dad, I can't do any of those ideas quickly!" he said as the painful truth sank in.

I agreed. "Only in the movies is it easy to make money. In the real world it takes work. I told you to save money for the things you wanted, but you were too quick to spend instead of saving. Sean, you invested in the wrong CDs!"

Three months later, Sean came to me with his plan. "I've figured out how I am going to get my car."

"How?" I asked with a somewhat supportive smile.

"I'm going to write a book. You've written books, and you've made money on those books. I can do that."

The earnest look in his eye gave me a bit of a start. As a parent, tired of the sixteen-year struggle, I was tempted to say, "It would be nice if you could start with your term paper!" But that would be far from motivational, and as a motivational speaker, how could I say such a thing to my son? After all, underneath it all, I wanted him to be successful. If he didn't get a career or make enough money, I could be stuck with this young man for the rest of my life. Plus, inside I felt a glimmer of hope that matched his own. With a smile, I asked, "OK, what is your book going to be about?"

"I'm going to write a book on my favorite family lectures."

Yes, it hung there for a moment, penetrating my mind in stages. I mustered a three-word prompt, "Favorite family lectures?"

"Yea, you have given me so many lectures, and some of them are really good ones. They're even funny! And I know from school that most parents don't know what to say to their kids. So I'm going to collect all the ones you've told me, interview the kids at school to get some of the other best ones, and then I'm going to write the book. We have a huge market because I think parents are so busy that they don't have time to lecture. I'm going to number the lectures so that all a parent has to do is to hand the kid the book and say, 'Read number 22!'"

I smiled a somewhat surprised but proud smile, "That just may sell!" He launched for the advantage. "In fact, I want you to write it with me because you can sell a lot of books!"

"Ah, a strategic alliance. Sure, you partner with me, and I'm the one who writes the book."

"No, I'll do the interviewing, and we'll write it together."

Three years later we had our first book. Before

the book was finished, Sean had already gotten a part-time job, saved his money, and bought a used car from his grandmother. After becoming an author, however, he did get a better car!

He's now married, working and living on his own, and we have finished writing two books together. The first, *Secrets of Life Every Teen Needs to Know,* sold more than ten thousand copies for Joy Publishing. Our second book, entitled, *Can I Have the Keys to the Car? How Parents and Teens Can Talk about the Things That Really Matter,* is designed to help parents, teens, and church youth leaders to make a lasting difference together.

The books remain lasting legacies that will continue to make a difference to parents and teens alike, but the biggest legacy is what happened in our own relationship. As a father and son team, we had a reason to have conversations about the important things in life that few parents and teens ever get to have. We are both better for it.

Irrespective of what heights of success Sean achieves, I am proud. Sean is a good man, a man of character and faith. He is a man who knows that the Ten Commandments are not the Ten Suggestions. He and his wonderful wife, Nicole, are both active in their church and have a strong faith in God.

Could a parent ask for anything more? And to think, it all started by caring enough to say no. You can't always give your children the biggest gifts. The best gifts are lessons earned on the backs of their own hard work, so they, like good stewards through the centuries, can learn to work the gifts God has given them.

◆ ◆ ◆

The Florida Snowman

Marti (Martha Ellen) Suddarth

"What do you want for Christmas?" my mother-in-law asked. Janet's voice was as cheerful long distance from Florida as it was in person.

"Snow!" I wailed, "I want some snow!"

I was young and newly married. Two and a half months before, my husband and I had moved ten hours away from my family in Indiana, to Macon, Georgia. Now, even though the calendar read, "November," the thermometer outside read, "July." I was hot, humid, homesick, and facing a warm and snowless Christmas.

Janet laughed nervously, my husband turned the conversation to his new job, and I felt even more miserable than before.

A few weeks later, Janet's annual Christmas box arrived. Inside we found several nicely wrapped gifts for each of us, a new Christmas ornament, Janet's traditional box of English Toffee, and a small box marked, "To Marti . . . Open right away." I did. I laughed so hard that I cried.

"What is it?" asked my husband as I turned the box for him to see.

Inside was a small, plastic snow dome without any snow. Instead, floating in the clear water were several little plastic lumps of coal, a teeny plastic carrot, and a tiny plastic top hat. At the bottom of the white base—in black letters—were the words, "Florida Snowman."

That Christmas and every Christmas since, the Florida Snowman has held a place of honor among my decorations, a symbol of my mother-in-law's love. Janet knew that sometimes the gift of laughter is the best gift one can give.

What Did You Make for Supper?

Elena Dorothy Bowman

Sometimes being the only girl in a family with five kids can be fun; at other times it can be disastrous. For instance, when I was around ten, my parents had to go out suddenly, putting me in charge of dinner. So I had to cook for myself and my four brothers: Bob, Alfred, Richard, and Tommy.

I had no idea what to make. My brothers were no help in that department either.

"Do what Ma does," they chorused. "She always comes up with something."

"Thanks a lot," I answered. "That's easier said than done. Ma can look at an empty refrigerator and bare cupboards and come up with a delicious meal. Me? If it's not there to begin with, we'll all starve!"

My brothers went on their merry way and left me to 'surprise' them. Since my brothers did not have any suggestions or offer to help, I decided on hot dogs, beans, and brown bread. That seemed like a pretty good meal to me.

Well, with the hot dogs and beans on the stove and the brown bread in the oven, all at low temperatures, I went off to read the book I had put down in order to start supper. I promptly forgot what was cooking on the stove.

Several hours later my brothers came bounding into the house crying, "What did you make for supper?"

Parroting my mother, I answered, "Go wash first!"

I set the table as my brothers washed, and when they came into the kitchen and started to serve themselves, I cut the brown bread into slices, placed two slices on each of their plates, then served them the beans, giving the older ones a little more than the younger ones.

When I removed the cover from the pan holding the hot dogs, I stifled a scream. My mind could not fathom what was in the pan, and I caught myself desperately trying to remember what I had put in there.

Hoping my brothers wouldn't notice the difference, I replaced the cover on the pan, put the pan on a hot pad on the kitchen table, and waited—praying, as I sat down to join them, that it would all be over soon.

Alfred was the first to reach over and uncover the pan. Ashen-faced, I watched helplessly. Al looked into the pan and then looked back up to me. He smiled. "Oh," he said, "you made hearts!"

My other brothers stood up and leaned over to look in the pan. The water had boiled off, the skin had split, and the hot dogs were turned inside out and curled into a ball covering the bottom of the pan. Packed tightly together, the newly created culinary delight actually did look like hearts.

With a grateful sigh and a smile for Alfred, I watched as my brothers sat down and dug in. Al bit into a hot dog, chewed for a moment or two, looked at me, and winked. "They taste like hearts too!" he grinned.

"Thanks," I whispered as I, too, relaxed and dug in.

After dinner Al helped me clear the table. His eyes crinkling with laughter and with a grin on his face, he mirthfully asked, "When are you going to make hearts again!"

Momentarily caught off guard, I stared at him in disbelief. Then realizing he was joking, I swiped at him with my dish towel but missed. We then grabbed hold of each other and laughed hilariously.

What's Your Name?

Joanne Wallace

I have a friend, a pastor's wife, who is working on some self-esteem issues. Her husband, the head pastor of a church, is a very outgoing, gregarious personality who enjoys greeting everyone after church. My friend is somewhat reserved, sometimes shy, and finds it hard to laugh freely. Lately she has been praying about gaining a better sense of humor and learning to relax more.

Today she called to tell me that the Lord was answering her prayers. At the end of last week's church service, she and her husband were standing at the church door greeting people as they left. Since it is a growing church with a large congregation, many first-time people were at the service. As each person came close to her husband, he would reach out a hand to him or her and say, "Now, what's your name?"

In the midst of all the people milling around him, he forgot that his wife was standing next to him. Without really looking at her, he then turned to his wife and said, "Now, what's your name?"

With a big smile on her face and a twinkle in her eye she sweetly replied, "Remember, I'm the one you slept with last night."

Peals of laughter were heard from the regular attendees who had gathered around the newcomers. The pastor looked slightly shocked and completely taken by surprise. As quickly as he could recover his senses, he started assuring everyone that she was his wife!

My friend told me about how good it felt to be able to have a sense of humor and tease her husband. She walked around the rest of that day feeling better about herself. Her husband, although surprised at this new side of his usually shy wife, has been delighted to see her relax. They have been laughing together about the incident, and they both have a new appreciation for each other.

6
Love Forgives

To err is human, to forgive, divine.
Pope—Essay on Criticism

Letters to Death Row

Linda Evans Shepherd

"Linda," my mother's voice crackled across the phone line, "Sharon Cain disappeared last weekend!"

I felt a sudden sickness in the pit of my stomach. "You're kidding!" I said, "I saw Sharon Saturday. What happened?"

My mother paused. "That's the day she was reported missing. Apparently she and her husband were walking home from the Gateway Shopping Center after their car broke down."

I sat down, overwhelmed. "That's where I saw her," I stammered. "It . . . it never occurred to me she needed help!"

I hung up the phone, replaying the events of Saturday afternoon.

It had been a hot drive from Denton, Texas, to Beaumont. I sat in our red Nova at a Mobil gas station while my husband paid the attendant. As I sat, I noticed Sharon and her husband as they walked from the shopping center parking lot into the gas station lot. I reached out of my open car window and waved. "Sharon," I called.

She didn't hear me.

I pushed open the heavy door and leaned over the car toward her. "Sharon!"

She never looked up. Suddenly, feeling like I was intruding, I ducked back to rest on my black vinyl seat and watched the pair stride past me. I studied the set of Sharon's jaw and noticed her arms were tight across her chest. *It looks like those two are having an argument,* I decided. *But why would they be walking through the gas station? Surely they're not thinking of walking down the freeway.*

That's when I noticed the steak house across the road from us. *That's it. They're going to lunch.*

Later I learned that shortly after passing me, Sharon's husband had sprinted ahead of her to jog down the freeway, planning to return for his wife with their other car. Meanwhile, a stranger accelerated toward Sharon. When he saw her walking alone, he screeched to a halt, swung open the car door, and yanked her inside by her long brown hair. Then he drove to an isolated beach on the Texas Gulf Coast. After brutalizing her, he abandoned her—leaving her to die buried alive in the sand.

Over the next few days, the ugly facts played over and over in my mind. The more I thought about them, the more furious I became with myself for not capturing Sharon's attention when I had called out to her. God had put them directly in my path, and I had blown it.

I didn't know! I argued with my conscience. *I couldn't have known Sharon was in danger.* In a sense, I was also a victim of this senseless tragedy.

I spent the next few nights in sleeplessness, turning the blame and anger from myself to Sharon's murderer. Months later, when Thomas Wilson was tried and sentenced to die by electrocution, I was elated. I believed even hell was too good for this man. Over time my bitterness only intensified.

But then one Sunday morning, I listened as our silver-haired pastor spoke from Mark 11:25, "And when you stand praying, if you hold anything against anyone, forgive him, so that your Father in heaven may forgive you your sins" (NIV).

That message shocked me. *This couldn't possibly apply to me and my hatred for Sharon's killer, could it, Lord?* I already knew the answer. *It isn't fair,* I silently screamed. *That man had no right to rob Sharon of her life! I can't believe you would want me to forgive him after what he did!*

I wrestled silently for months, contemplating the monstrous wrong committed against Sharon, her friends, and her family. I even mourned for the children she would never bear. Thomas Wilson's actions were unjustifiable, and therefore, I concluded, unforgivable.

As I curled on my blue floral sofa one evening, a question came to mind: *To receive God's forgiveness, must one's sin always be accompanied by a good excuse?*

In one painful moment, I knew I had to forgive Thomas Wilson—regardless of his crime—with or without an excuse.

My heart rebelled as my mind made a decision. It would be hard to give up my hatred; it was like exchanging a custom-fitted garment for one much too big. Even so, I weakly told the Lord that with his help I was willing to try to forgive this man, though it seemed far beyond my ability.

My first problem was how. *How does one go about forgiving the unforgivable? And how would I know if I'd succeeded?* Though several years had passed, the mere mention of Thomas Wilson's name still sent shivers down my spine.

Before I could take any action, I received word that Thomas Wilson had been executed. I couldn't help but feel relief that this episode of my life had ended—or so I thought.

One day, while reading in the sunlit bay window of my new Colorado home, I saw an item about an organization called Death Row Support Project. I stared at the view of the snow-capped Long's Peak on the western horizon and began to feel the Lord prompting me to test my so-called forgiveness on a real person.

"Don't do it, Linda," my mother cautioned. "Think of the victims' families."

"I sympathize with them," I agreed, "but I have to find out how big God's forgiveness really is."

After much trepidation and a few crumpled starts, I wrote a letter, asking for the name of a death-row inmate with whom I could correspond. I secretly hoped I would get the name of someone whose crime would be easy to forgive.

When the letter arrived from the project, I opened it with trembling hands. I was shocked to read the name of Johnny Lee Simpson, a convicted murderer from my own hometown of Beaumont, Texas.

My mother was horrified, "He killed two women during a bank robbery! First he shared a cup of coffee with them, then he shot each of them in the head!"

Pregnant with my first child, I, too, was appalled that this man had killed two young mothers. I didn't want to forgive Johnny either.

With difficulty, I began writing to Johnny. The sensitive replies that came from this intelligent, fifty-year-old convict amazed me.

"Who would have thought my life would have turned out like this?" Johnny wrote. "There was a time when I taught a boys' Sunday school class. But I've turned my back on all that. Don't pity me. I've made my own choices. I want to die and go to hell to pay the debt I owe society."

Through our correspondence, Johnny shared in my joy over the birth of my daughter, Laura, and grieved with me when she was injured in a terrible car crash. "I sat up all night in my cell and thought solely of Laura and you in that hospital. Before daylight, I got the definite feeling that Laura was going to be fine and would grow into a lovely woman. You are not alone."

Somehow, it was easier for me to forgive Johnny than it had been to forgive Thomas Wilson, not because he deserved it, but because God's hand was moving in our lives. I could feel God's love and compassion for him, just as he had felt God's love and compassion for us.

One March morning, Johnny sent bad news, "An hour ago, I received another date of execution for May the 3rd. As I have turned my back on my own faith, I shall not be a hypocrite and ask for God's forgiveness. Please understand."

"But Johnny," I wrote in my next letter, "none of us deserve God's forgiveness. Can't you see that God will pardon your sins, if you only ask?"

His letter was a blow, "Many long and lost years ago I had a deep and abiding faith, which I alone destroyed. In so doing, I destroyed myself. I cannot look back. I will die without God."

With Johnny's execution date only weeks away, I yearned to see him experience God's forgiveness. If only I could make him understand!

As I sat at my typewriter, trying to define God's forgiveness for Johnny into words, the enormity of God's grace and mercy became real to me. With great anticipation and prayer, I mailed my letter and waited for a response. Later I learned that my letter never reached him. Instead, God proved himself to Johnny without my help.

"Very late Thursday night," Johnny wrote. "I had my back turned to the bars . . . listening to all the yelling and cussing, but suddenly, I did not hear a sound, only a voice within me saying, 'You shall not die, there are things you have to do.'

"Later, my Bible dropped from the shelf onto my bunk. I picked it up and it fell open to Colossians 1:13–14: 'For he has rescued us from the dominion of darkness and brought us into the kingdom of the Son He loves, in whom we have redemption, the forgiveness of sins.'

"I understand now. Jesus has forgiven even me, even though I don't deserve it. I'm in His Kingdom now."

I read the letter with joy, realizing that while I was in the process of becoming Johnny's friend, the Lord was totally removing the last traces of bitterness from my spirit over the murder of my friend Sharon. I was wonderfully free!

And Johnny? Today, after a year of leading a Bible study in his cell block and writing letters to encourage children on a hospital's cancer ward, he's faced his final execution date. He's with his Creator now, a forgiven man. Someday, when I cross over to heaven, I will give Johnny a great big hug. I'll probably even say, "I told you so."

A Piece of Forgiveness

Carmen Leal-Pock

When Dave and I went through premarital counseling, I remember being asked about my greatest fear concerning our forthcoming marriage. "Having to care for Dave when he gets old is my greatest fear," I said. "I don't do 'sick,' and I want to die before Dave does so I won't have to care for him."

The second question I remember involved my expectations for the marriage. I had many; some of them included the expectation of a partner for decades to come, someone to be a role model for my children, a handyman to fix my dilapidated house, and a partner to earn enough to make us comfortable. I didn't think any of my expectations were unrealistic.

When Dave was diagnosed with Huntington's disease three years into our marriage, I, of course, knew that my worst fears had been realized and that my expectations would not be met. I was angry—not so much at Dave as with the disease and the circumstances. What could I do but go on? So we went on, finding solutions to problems and doing the best we could.

One solution involved uprooting my teenage sons and moving to a different state. It was hard, but I didn't see other options at the time. Knowing that no nursing home in Hawaii would take a person with HD, I realized I would probably move eventually, and it may as well be now. I was angry at having to pull my children away from the only home they had ever known, but we would adjust.

After six months of struggling to make a life for ourselves in Florida, Dave made a stunning announcement. One morning he woke up and told me he had a confession to make. "I knew I was sick when I asked you to marry me," he said.

"You knew you had Huntington's?" I gasped.

"No, I knew I was sick. I thought I had multiple sclerosis."

When we married, Dave's mother was living in another state. She was in the final stages of what he thought was multiple sclerosis.

"I don't care what initials you put on it, MS or HD. It doesn't really matter; you lied to me," I yelled.

How could he not tell me something of this magnitude, especially when I had told him my biggest fears, my greatest expectations? Our marriage had been a lie from day one, and I could never forgive him.

Even though Dave depended on me to feed him and provide for most of his needs, I told him, with contempt, "I have to sort things out in my mind. I can't be around you until I'm ready. You'll just have to starve!" With that, I got out of bed and left the room. Of course Dave didn't starve, but I had a choice to make. How would I handle Dave's lie?

Undeniably, it was wrong. Yet I didn't know if he had lied by omission because his mind was already severely affected or because he was afraid of being alone. Maybe he lied because he loved me and feared my rejecting him. I had certainly given him every reason to believe that I would not have married him had I known he was sick because I told him how much I hated the thought of caring for a sick person.

Over the next few weeks I cared for Dave and was civil to him, but just barely. I spoke with a pastor at church and cried out my anguish to my on-line support group. My ladies' Bible study group also listened to my dilemma. I knew in my heart that there was absolutely no way I would have married someone with a disease as crippling as MS, let alone one with even greater ramifications, like HD. I certainly would have never dragged my children into this mess that had caused me to lose everything as I continued to rack up piles of debt.

I received advice from many, and the vast majority were appalled at Dave's disclosure. They urged me to find a nursing home for him, get a divorce, and begin my life again. The temptation to do just that was never far from my mind. After all, hadn't our marriage been built on lies? I had no moral obligation to remain, provided I made sure he was taken care of. During this time, I found myself becoming more short-tempered with my children and more unhappy with myself as the battle within me raged.

Praying and asking God for direction one day, I realized that although I had not told Dave a lie about my health when we married, I was also responsible for areas of failure in our marriage. In retelling the situation with Dave to others, I had made Dave's indiscretion worse and worse in my mind. I had fashioned Dave into a liar of the worst type who had sought me out intentionally to destroy my life.

Of course, that wasn't true at all. Dave was a desperately sick man with a disease that had already begun to rob him of his ability to make right decisions.

He made a mistake, but that did not mean he didn't deserve love and should be abandoned. I knew that if I chose to walk away from him, God would still love me and forgive me. But would that be the right thing to do?

At that moment I forgave Dave and recommitted myself to give him the best care I could. My struggle to care for him has been difficult, but with God's help, it has been devoid of bitterness. Not only have I found peace, but I have rekindled my love for the man I am losing.

Anguish in the Night

Jerry B. Jenkins

When Raymond was awakened by the phone after midnight one Saturday morning, his wife didn't stir. As he made his way to the living room, his thoughts raced to his two married sons and a daughter still in college.

He hoped for a wrong number. Phone calls in the night rarely bring good news. He offered a sleepy, muffled, octave-lower-than-usual, "Hello?"

All he heard was sobbing. He prayed silently, "Father, give me strength for whatever is wrong."

"Daddy?" the female voice managed.

"Yes," Raymond answered, his voice thick from sleep. His daughter just sobbed. Raymond whispered so as not to disturb his wife, "Honey, what is it?"

"Oh, Daddy!" she said, fighting for control. He waited. "Daddy, I'm sorry."

Raymond hoped it was only a failed test, a failed class, a failed semester. She cried and cried. "Daddy?" she said.

"I'm here," he said.

"Daddy, I'm pregnant."

Raymond's heart sank. How could it be? He and his wife had raised their children in love, in the church, from the Bible. Each member of the family had a personal relationship with Christ, and each had an unusual ability to interact with the others. The kids had always been open about their struggles and temptations.

Raymond didn't even know his daughter had a boyfriend. Was the father a new love? Had she been forced? Was it someone he knew? With the phone pressed to his ear, his free hand covering his eyes, he prayed silently for strength, the right words, the right response. He was brokenhearted.

Raymond had always feared he might explode in anger and embarrassment over such news. Yet now he found himself overcome with sympathy, pity, and protectiveness for his precious child, still in the bloom of youth.

His daughter—clearly distressed, broken, repentant—begged for forgiveness. Raymond didn't ask for details. "We love you," he said through his tears. "We forgive you."

He was on the phone more than a half-hour, then sat crying until dawn when his wife padded out to hear the news. They went through the day in their pajamas, hardly eating, working on a letter. It assured their daughter that they would always be there for her and the baby and that they would be available to counsel her or to support her decision on what to do about the father. The post office promised the letter would be delivered early Monday morning. The waiting was torture.

Raymond prayed all weekend that God would somehow erase history, would put things back the way they had been.

On Monday morning a pale, bleary-eyed Raymond went to work. Midmorning he took a call from his daughter. "Daddy," she said, laughing, "what in the world is this letter all about?"

It had not been a joke. Not a crank call. It had been a wrong number—a tragic mistake in the middle of the night—two people in turmoil thinking they knew to whom they were talking. Raymond spent the rest of the day vainly trying to help the phone company determine where the call could have originated. He didn't want a girl, thinking her father had forgiven her, racing home only to find that he knew nothing about her situation.

Raymond, an old acquaintance, is a saint. He admits that was the most traumatic experience he's ever had, but he's grateful that it made him sensitive to parents who do receive such unbearable news. "For forty-eight hours, my wife and I ached."

In a way, though, God answered Raymond's prayer. With the Monday call, everything was put back the way it had been—everything except Raymond. He will never be the same again.

A Severe Mercy

As told to Janice Byrd

I was a precocious boy and prone to mischief, at least according to my mother who was the disciplinarian in my home. The severest punishment I ever got, however, was not from my mother but from my gentle father.

Many people said my dad reminded them of Jimmy Stewart. He was tall and trim with the same side-part hairstyle and boyish grin. After the movie *It's a Wonderful Life* was released in 1946, folks in our town, McKinney, Texas, teased him by calling him George Bailey, partly because he worked at the First Savings and Loan and partly because the resemblance was uncanny.

My dad, Clifford Byrd, was the epitome of a family man. He worked hard without the benefit of a formal education, believed in the American dream, and understood that he owed something to his country and community. He enlisted during the War, despite the fact that he had a wife and a new baby. His two sons were the pride of his life.

All of my family was involved in Boy Scouting, even Mom. Dad was our scoutmaster. The First Baptist Church of McKinney elected him a deacon year after year, and his banking customers were accustomed to hearing him speak openly about his faith.

Bob, my older brother, was like Dad—orderly, deliberate, and predictable. When Bob left for college, however, Dad and I were able to forge a new relationship based on our complimentary and contrasting temperaments. I was more like my intuitive and impulsive mother, which sometimes caused problems between us.

I loved to walk down to the town square after school and spend time with Dad at the office. Mom didn't get home from her secretarial job until after five, so I would have at least an hour to run the adding machine, oversee a cash register close-out, or listen to some anxious patron wanting a loan. (In his twenty years with the savings and loan, Clifford never failed to work out some kind of a deal to get folks the money they needed, and he never had to foreclose on anyone.) True enough, Mom had given me explicit instructions to go straight home after school, but Dad was content to keep our secret.

I didn't always make it to the square, however. Occasionally, my buddies and I would gather at the hardware store or hang out at the drugstore when money was available for a soda. Most of the time we guys were hatching plans to come up with a little spending money.

Just about every gift I ever asked for when I was a kid was a means to that end. For Christmas I had requested a portrait camera so I could photograph my friends and sell the prints to their delighted mothers. Summers were always best for my entrepreneurial activities. Long ago I had graduated from the proverbial lemonade stand and had taken to hawking the leftovers from supper the night before. When I was four years old, I took my red wagon around the block, selling tap water out of a gallon jug.

I don't exactly remember the details of how it happened, but somehow a friend's yard caught fire late one afternoon after school as the two of us worked on our cooking merit badge. Mom was called at work, and she was mad! "I told you to go home after school," was all she said on our long ride home.

To this day, the memory of my chastisement has overshadowed my remembrance of the crime. Mother was so upset that she banished me to my room without so much as a tongue-lashing. *That was a first!* "Your father will have to deal with this," she coldly admonished.

Never had Mom failed to administer justice when it came time to teach me a lesson. On the other hand, my dad was an unknown quantity when it came to implementing punishment. Exiled in my room, I rehearsed my explanation. I truly was repentant, but mostly I was sorry that my adored and idolized father was going to have to find out about "the accident."

Usually I just took my mother's corporal punishment, if not willingly, at least with a sense of relief that Dad would never have to know. I secretly prayed that Mother would change her mind and storm into my room and get it over with, as usual. It was not to be!

All too soon I heard the sound of my father's car pulling into the driveway, my parents' whispers from the living room, and the footsteps that eventually found me. We went into the bathroom to talk. Dad sat on the commode, and I sat on the side of the tub. There was never a question about my guilt. I was very contrite, and there was no argument about the horrible consequences of my disobedience.

"This is so bad," Dad stuttered. "There's going to have to be a very severe punishment. Stand up, turn around, and hold onto the shower door," he directed.

As I braced myself, I heard Dad stand up and loosen his belt buckle. I heard the sound of the folded belt whizzing through the air, and I anticipated—then heard—the striking blow, but I felt nothing! Instinctively, I turned around. My gentle father's hand was poised in midair, ready to once again thrash his own leg.

"No!" I protested.

All of our past and all our future hung there in that present moment. "This time I took your punishment," Dad stammered. "You have been given mercy instead of what you deserve. We would have quickly forgotten a spanking, but we'll never forget what mercy felt like."

Though it's been close to forty years ago, I can still vividly recall my father's tear-streaked face and the disappointment in his eyes that day. I remember it most when I look into the pleading face of my own son. It is then that I know—it was a severe mercy.

Red Rooster

Doris Smalling

"Teacher, are you saying that even if someone does me dirty, I should ask for forgiveness, too, and if I don't, I'm disobeying God?"

"Yes, Jamie, that's what this lesson says."

"Is that crazy, or what? I say that's not fair."

Twelve-year-old Jamie crossed his arms over his chest and slouched down in his chair. The seven older junior high students in my Sunday school class looked at him and at me, scrutinizing us intently.

"I know it doesn't seem fair, Jamie, but that's what God tells us to do, and he knows best—always. Maybe if I tell you a story of two girls and a little red rooster, you'll understand better. Want to hear it?"

All the students responded eagerly, except Jamie. I knew he was interested, though, when he pulled his knees up for a chin rest, creating his favorite "listening position."

"You see, this is a *real* story. I know it's true because I was one of the girls, and my sister Elaine was the other."

As I spoke I carefully unwrapped the item on my lap. I held the little red rooster up so they could see it.

"I'm going to let the little red rooster travel around among you while I tell you the story of how it changed my life." I continued speaking.

"You see, one day Elaine became very angry with me—so angry, in fact, she swore she'd never speak to me again."

"What made her so mad?" Jamie asked, looking up from his "chin rest."

"That was the problem, Jamie. I didn't know why she got so mad at me. For months—actually until I graduated and started college—I lived in the same house with a sister who refused to speak to me. She wouldn't tell any of us why she was mad—not even Mom. Even when Mom had us do things together, she'd just do her work and never speak a word. Dad even ordered her to tell us what was wrong, or he'd put her on restriction. She took her punishment rather than talk to me."

"Gosh, she really was mad, wasn't she?" Jamie sat up straighter. "What did you do?"

"Finally, I got so disgusted that I got mad too, and I said I didn't care if we made up or not."

"I had that happen to me once, teacher. I ain't going to tell you what I did though."

Curiously, the other students didn't laugh at Jamie as they usually did.

"Those things do hurt, don't they, Jamie?"

"What did you do, Mrs. Smalling?" several students asked.

"You bought the little red rooster," Jamie exclaimed, making a *V* sign with his fingers.

"You're right, Jamie, that I did, but not right away. I did what I should have done long before. I went to my pastor. I didn't think he'd have time for me, but he listened to me and helped me think things through."

"Did he tell you to buy the red rooster?" David asked.

"No, David, but the red rooster came as the result of his telling me I had to pray for guidance—pray without ceasing—and he said that if I read Ephesians 4:32 I'd know what I had to do. Will one of you read that verse for us?"

"Be ye kind one to another, tender-hearted, forgiving one another, even as God for Christ's sake hath forgiven you" (KJV). David's voice seemed unusually subdued. He seemed to be wondering.

"Tell us what happened after that, Mrs. Smalling," he said quietly.

"David, I knew I had to forgive my sister even though I hadn't done anything to her. That sounds strange, doesn't it?"

"Yeah," Jamie interjected. "I still don't get it—you hadn't done anything to her. She should ask you to forgive her!" Jamie sounded almost petulant.

"I thought so, too, for awhile, Jamie. Then a thought struck me. It hit me like I'd been belted by an El Niño windstorm. Suddenly, I realized that Christ didn't argue about who was right or wrong when he died for me on the cross. He simply took my place because he loved me. He didn't do anything wrong, and he loved us enough to die like that. And I loved my sister very much, so I had to find a way to let her know I was sorry for hurting her even if I didn't know what I'd done."

The students sat quietly—even Jamie. I perceived a glimpse of understanding stirring. "That day I felt so sorry for Elaine. How she must have hurt. I know that's the only reason she wanted to hurt me. I prayed that God would show me a way to reach her."

Jamie sat upright, raising his hand. "Did you find a way, teacher?"

"Yes, Jamie, I did. God put the little red rooster right in my path."

"How?" Several students asked at the same time.

"About a week later, my college roommate and I were walking along the pier in Long Beach, California. There, in the window of an international gift shop, stood this little red rooster. It seemed he beckoned to me. 'Look at that rooster,' I shouted to my friend, 'my sister collects roosters. Let's go see it.'"

My voice conveyed the excitement I felt that day. The students felt it, too, and took turns touching and petting the little red rooster.

"Not only did I know Elaine collected roosters," I told them, "but I learned that red roosters are a symbol of courage and love in some South American countries. The clerk said this one was from Peru, designed by native Peruvian Indians, and it symbolized love.

"When I saw it there in the window, I turned to my friend. She knew about Elaine. 'I'm going to send this rooster to Elaine,' I told her 'and see if she acknowledges it.'"

Jamie couldn't wait. "Did she acknowledge it?"

In spite of a promise I made to myself not to become emotional, my voice choked.

"Yes, Jamie, she did. She had recently married. As soon as she received my gift and my letter, she called me—on the Friday night before Easter."

"What did she say?" Marla asked quietly.

"She used my childhood nickname, and she said,

'Dorrie, Dorrie, you don't know how many times I've started to call and tell you how sorry I am for listening to lies. I learned the awful things you're supposed to have said were lies, and I'm so ashamed. I'm most ashamed because I should have known you wouldn't hurt me like that. I shouldn't have jumped to conclusions, but I did. I'm so sorry.'"

Jamie sat quietly, saying nothing.

"Elaine told me she thought it wouldn't hurt as much to leave things alone the way they were because she was afraid I'd tell her I hated her if she called me. She said she couldn't bear to hear me say that. I remember her saying, 'I don't understand how you could forgive me enough to send this precious little red rooster, but I thank God you did. Dorrie, can you ever forgive me? I love you.'"

The students watched intently as Marla brought the little red rooster to me. She laid it in my lap.

Jamie stood up. "I have a question to ask, Mrs. Smalling."

I nodded. "Go ahead, Jamie."

"You said you sent the rooster to Elaine. How come you have it now?"

I took a deep breath. "Remember I told you Elaine called me on a Friday night before Easter Sunday?"

"Yes," they answered.

"On Easter Sunday afternoon, Elaine's husband called to tell me she'd had a brain hemorrhage. She never regained consciousness. When I went to her funeral, he gave me the little red rooster. Almost as if she knew, she had told him that if anything ever happened to her, he must return the little rooster to me and tell me how much she loved me and she'd be waiting for me in heaven."

Jamie came to stand by my chair. He stroked the little red rooster.

"Mrs. Smalling," he asked, "I don't think it's crazy anymore. Do you think God will help me talk to my father again? I said some mean things to him."

"Yes, Jamie, I know he will. Just ask him." I stood up to give him a hug. Tears stung my eyes as students lined up to exchange hugs with me and with each other and to whisper their promises to give 'little red roosters' to those who need to be forgiven.

"You'd Better Be Good"

Marlene Bagnull

Sunday's paper was fat with ads for last-minute Christmas shoppers. Big bold letters warned there were only a few days left to buy gifts for loved ones. *And to get everything else done,* I thought grimly. But it wasn't just time pressures that were getting to me. It was everything.

I remembered my childhood and how my mother used to get irritable as the holidays approached. "I'd like to forget all about Christmas," she'd grumble. I thought she was awful for feeling that way. Now I had become just like her.

"Oh God, what's wrong with me?" I wept. "I should be happy. You've blessed me with a good husband and beautiful children. We're healthy. We have a nice home. We've seen you working in our lives this past year."

I knew I could and should go on to list our many, many blessings, but other emotions that were too powerful to suppress kept surfacing—anger, hurt, guilt. No matter how hard I tried, I felt like I would never be able to measure up to what God and others expected of me. For some reason the coming of Christmas intensified those feelings.

My eye caught the words at the top of an advertisement: "Toys for good girls and boys."

Suddenly a torrent of painful, buried memories flooded over me. "Santa won't come if you're not a good girl," my mother and father began threatening as soon as the stores decorated for Christmas.

'I'd try, really try, to be good, but I never felt I was good enough. On Christmas Eve I would go to bed filled with fear that there would be only coal in my stocking the next morning.

I remembered getting walking dolls and a train set, but I couldn't remember ever feeling that they gave me those gifts because they loved me. I couldn't remember being hugged—especially by my father.

What I did remember were his slaps across my face and the way he locked me in his bedroom (I didn't have a room of my own). I cried alone for hours before he finally opened the door. When he did, he never told me it was OK now. He never told me that he forgave me or that he loved me.

I wanted to suppress the memories once again, but God wouldn't let me. "It's time for you to be free of them," he gently said.

"But how, Lord?" I wept.

"Can you forgive him?" he asked.

"I don't know," I replied as I realized how those childhood experiences had shaped my entire life. No wonder I felt so much anger, hurt, and guilt. For years I had been trying to be good enough to make people love me—to make God love me. But I had never made it and never would.

"Nor do you have to, my child," I felt him say. "You don't have to earn my love. It's my Christmas gift to you."

"But I can't give you anything, Lord," I said. "I can't even live the way you want me to live. I fail you so miserably."

"No, those are the lies you've been believing for too long. Listen to my words of truth."

What is truth? I thought. *Did my father ever love me?* I'd never know. He died when I was twelve. As far as I knew, he never accepted the Lord. I didn't dare to hope I'd someday see him in heaven.

My father had been seriously ill most of my life. He was hospitalized more times than I could remember with insulin shock, heart trouble, and a collapsed lung. I was never allowed to visit him.

When he came home, I had to be super good—especially the time he had a blood clot in his leg. That time they didn't put him in the hospital, but my mother warned me that if I wasn't good—if I got him upset—the blood clot could go to his heart and kill him.

The truth! Suddenly I saw it. *I wasn't the problem! His health was the problem. I probably wasn't anymore naughty than any other child. My parents were just under so much stress. They didn't mean to hurt me. And they didn't mean to withhold their love.*

And, I realized, *I cannot continue to withhold my love or my forgiveness.*

"God, I want to be free," I prayed. "Help me to forgive him. Mother too. Take away the anger, the hurt, and the guilt that have been festering in me for so long."

I felt God performing surgery on my soul. I knew I'd never again need to be driven by those you'd-better-be-good threats. I had received the best Christmas gift possible. God loved me so much that he sent his only Son to die on the cross for my sins. He had forgiven me for every time I failed him. And he would keep me from "slipping and falling away" and bring me, "sinless and perfect, into his glorious presence with mighty shouts of everlasting joy" (Jude 25 TLB).

7
Love Befriends

Love Listens

Love listens—using silence to talk
louder than a thousand words—
bending near the sick one,
focusing attention on the need.

Looking as though there's
no one else
in the wide, wide world.
Except the one who needs to talk.

Love is watertight, never leaking the confidences
shared at midnight—or the dawn—
or in the middle of the day!
Time is irrelevant to love.

Love borrows wisdom from on high
passing on eternity's information
at the right time
and in the right way.

Love's ears are open to a shriek or groan,
complaints or angry shout.
It matters not—
No one listens like love.

Jill Briscoe

A Dress So Fine

Steve Wise

It was a Sunday summer morning, and as the family van rolled to a stop in the supermarket parking lot, everyone began their parts right on cue—Travis and Stacee fought over which page of the funnies should be read first and by whom, and Cathy turned the radio up a notch so that the tune would drown them out.

As I stepped through the store's automatic door, the familiar hope of a short line at the bakery counter sprang to mind. The plan was simple: three dozen doughnuts and a gallon of milk for my junior high Sunday school class, and back to the van. I would not even have to fully turn on my brain until I arrived at church. But as so often happens in seemingly humdrum pieces of life, things would change quickly.

She was third in line, and I took my place behind her and looked over her shoulder at the bakery clerk who was patiently taking a halting order from a youngster obviously overwhelmed by the delectable array of sweet-smelling choices. I sighed—a bit too loudly—and the woman turned and smiled at me, shaking her head as she pushed at her glasses with a forefinger. I returned the smile.

She was fortyish, with a spare face etched with lines that should not have been there, but somehow they did not detract from her pleasing countenance. Though once black, her hair retained only enough darkness to be a reminder of another time. There was

only the hint of makeup on her skin—a delicate pink-
ness to the cheeks and lipstick judiciously applied.

"If I was ten and in front of that glass, I probably
wouldn't do much better," she said, toying with a but-
ton on her dress.

I chuckled with her. "Me neither, I'm sure."

While her fingers played over the cloth, a small
square of masking tape caught my eye. It was stuck
high on the dress, above her collarbone and near the
open neck. My heart sank as I stole another glance and
saw the black-penned numerals glaring against the yel-
lowish backdrop of the tape: $4.00. She had obviously
purchased the dress at a yard sale and forgot to
remove the price tag from the garment.

We continued with our small talk, and I learned
that she, too, was making a doughnut run for a Sunday
school class at another church, but my mind was
beginning to focus on the task at hand—how to dis-
creetly rid this lady of something that would soon
become a source of embarrassment. In spite of my
mind's focus, I began to absorb the details of the dress
like some urbane fashion correspondent: light green
print; tiny flowers tied together in an endless vine;
white collar, rounded, lying flat; pearly buttons to the
waist; slightly puffed short sleeves with a white hem to
match the collar; two-inch-thick belt of the same material; knee-length hemline.

Save for the telltale square of tape, the dress
might well have been purchased at a good clothing
store. I thought of this woman's life as I talked with her,
and I looked more closely at her hands—unpolished
nails, jagged and worn short, prominent knuckles

white with the slightest flexion. I knew that the eight or nine dollars she was about to spend were hard-earned dollars and that she would spend them with Christian love.

We were bound then—this stranger in the bakery line and me, bound with a love made complete two thousand years ago by the Son of Man—bound with a love for kids' faces stuffed with doughnuts and cups of milk balanced precariously on Bibles.

Suddenly it was time for her to order, and I had yet to come up with a proper plan for ridding her of the price tag. There was simply no way to remove it without acknowledging what it was. She placed the doughnut boxes in her cart and wheeled around to say goodbye as she began to pass me. It was now or never.

"Excuse me," I said, "there's something on your dress."

My right hand darted for the curled upper edge of the tape and found its mark. As furiously as my fingers could move, I rolled the tape into a tiny ball and dropped it on the floor. Her right hand shot up to the spot on her dress, and she opened her mouth to speak, but the words would not come. She knew at once what I had done, and suddenly I felt foolish for what seemed a brazen intrusion into her life. But the feeling of guilt passed quickly with the return of her beautiful smile and pleasant voice. "Why . . . thank you . . . thank you very much." She touched my arm, almost a pat, and spoke her farewell. "God bless you, sir."

I have not seen the woman since. We moved to another area of town and no longer make our doughnut stops at that market. Hundreds of Sunday mornings have come and gone since that day, and I cannot honestly say that I would recognize her today, that is, unless she happened to be wearing a certain green print dress with a white flat collar—a dress so fine that I cannot forget it—and one whose price is unknown.

When God Spoke Dutch

Bonnie Compton Hanson

As our ship pulled away in a rain of confetti and flowers, my husband Don held up our eleven-month-old son. "Wave good-bye to Australia, Robin!"

Brilliant down-under sunshine sparkled on the harbor waters, the waving eucalyptus trees, and the proud towers and bridges of Sydney. Yes, we would miss our new friends down under, their delightful accents, expansive hospitality to us "Yanks," and unique way of life. But on that August day in 1960, our sorrow at leaving after a year's stay was tempered by the joy of returning. *Wait till Robin's grandparents see how big he is getting!*

Actually, we hadn't expected to return so soon. But I was now six months pregnant with our next child, and my health was deteriorating fast. Our doctor advised flying back to the States, but in those days air travel was far more expensive than sea travel. Fortunately, a Dutch liner was due to dock at Sydney the following week. More good luck: since Robin's first birthday wouldn't be for another week, his fare was free.

The bad news? Don and I wouldn't be able to room together. Only three berths remained vacant on the entire ship. Don would share a cabin with three other men, and Robin and I would share one with an eighty-six-year-old woman. How in the world would I keep my lively toddler out of an elderly woman's hair? Oh well, at least things couldn't get worse.

Then I took a look at my new cabin mate. Even on this warm, sunny day, she wore a long-sleeved, high-necked, full-length gown of thick black wool. With half a dozen woolen slips underneath! Even her black shoes were high-tops! A severe, silver bun topped her stern, deeply lined face. "*Goede morgen* (good morning)!" she welcomed me primly. *Oh, no! She doesn't even speak English!*

But when she saw Robin, she broke out into a radiant smile and reached out her long, wrinkled hands to his short, dimpled ones.

I expected him to pull back in fear. Instead, he rushed to her arms, and they were buddies the rest of the trip!

Although neither of us knew the other's language, she quickly caught on to Robin's name. Every morning she sang out, "*Goede morgen,* Robin!" And even though he wasn't a year old yet, he was soon saying, "*Goede morgen*" too!

She also read from her Dutch Bible every morning and evening, encouraged me to get out my English Bible and to find the same passage she had turned to. Then she would read one verse in Dutch, I would read the next in English, and so on until we had read a chapter together. She especially loved the Book of Psalms. Then we'd sing a familiar hymn or two from the Dutch hymnbook she always carried. I think they were even more beautiful when we sang them in two languages at once.

Then we would pray. She had shown me the names and pictures of her children and grandchildren she had been visiting in Australia. Though they lived far from her own home and customs, they were never far from her heart and prayers. And those still in the Netherlands who would greet her joyously when she completed her arduous journey. She always prayed for them all.

Soon I picked up a few Dutch words from her as she did English ones from me. And there in a stifling, cramped cabin, side by side on a hard wooden berth, we shared the warmest, most loving fellowship I have ever known with another Christian.

We shared fun times too. When I made Robin a bunny costume out of his pajamas for a children's party, she roared with delight. Then she offered him hearty congratulations on his first birthday.

Unfortunately, when going through the Panama Canal, with both the temperature and the humidity registering over one hundred, she became deathly ill. The ship doctor's order: take off some of those long, woolen petticoats!

Then, just as we neared Cuba, a great hurricane struck. For days our captain agonized over whether to keep trying to outsail the storm or take refuge on the Communist island.

Unfortunately, taking refuge in Cuba would have meant that the five American citizens on board (my family and two others) would have been immediately imprisoned by Fidel Castro. The captain chose to maintain his defensive maneuvering of the ship. This decision meant spending an extra week at sea and running dangerously low on supplies.

During this time, many children became ill, including Robin. My now-beloved cabin mate cared for him as if he had been her own grandchild, sitting up all night with me to tend to his fever and coughing.

Finally, we outlasted the storm. As we neared New York, my cabin mate joined us in watching the Statue of Liberty break into view. Soon we were docked, and our long trip was over.

Before we left the ship, my new friend prayed in Dutch for Don and me, Robin, and my yet unborn child. And then together, in our own languages, we all said the Lord's Prayer before we embraced one last time. We waved to her from the shore as she prepared to sail on to Europe and her home—alone.

That's how I learned that God speaks Dutch. And that there is something greater in the world than differences between cultures. Or languages. Or even years and age. It's called love.

I Will Focus on the Children

Nancy Bayless

When I volunteered to be a greeter at our church, I considered it a ministry. "I will focus on the children," I decided. So the first Sunday, that's what I did.

I first approached a tiny girl who lifted her mother's dress and went underneath it to avoid my gesture of friendship!

Next, a boy marched past, looking at the ground without acknowledging the fact that I existed.

My first Sunday as a greeter was a disaster. Parents were harried, having in some cases helped four youngsters to get dressed for church. They looked at me as a roadblock in their goal not to be late to church. Teenagers gazed at a spot above my head, and most of my friends entered through other doors.

On the second Sunday, the tiny girl made eye contact before she put her thumb in her mouth and pulled her mother's skirt across her face.

The marching boy came to a dead stop in front of me. He did not look at me or respond to my presence. His hair stood straight up with the encouragement of some styling gel, and he seemed to be waiting for something. "I like your hair," I told him. As if a switch had been turned, he marched down the hall.

Some of the adults relaxed long enough to smile and say, "Good morning!" A few of my friends changed their usual course and veered through my door with comforting hugs. A couple of teenagers and a babe in arms grinned at me.

I felt better.

During the following week, I thought about my ministry often. I imagined Jesus standing at the door of my heart. I remembered how he had knocked, then waited for me to let him in, but for years I had turned away. The third Sunday I continued my church greeting.

On my one-month anniversary the tiny girl reached up with tentative fingers to touch my hand.

The marching boy stopped and asked if I would like to feel his hair. I gently ran my hand over it and down the side of his face.

The fifth week the tiny girl patted my knee as she passed by, then turned and smiled at me with candle-light in her eyes.

The marching boy held up his fingers to give me five, then grabbed my hand and put it carefully on his hair.

My greeting ministry is now in its sixth month, and it is blooming. The tiny girl waves from the parking lot. Then she comes hopping up to me, holding out her foot so that I can marvel at her new lace socks.

The marching boy stands impatiently at my side. He butts his head against me, waiting for me to give him a hug.

Most of the children have let me into their little hearts. Little girls pirouette across the doormat so I can see how far their dresses twirl. Boys look me in the eye and grin when I admire their ties or jazzy shoes.

I get to wiggle loose teeth and to see the holes after the teeth have come out. Children show me their Bibles and ask me if I know the stories they are learning in

Sunday school. Many of the teenagers seem genuinely glad to see me on their way into church.

Fathers stop so that I can caress the soft cheeks of babies nestled against their necks. Others wait while toddlers reach up to be held in my arms.

As these children reach out to me, I remember the way I learned to reach out with childlike faith to God and ask him to take over my life. I remind myself that during all the years I ignored God, he waited at the door of my life and kept knocking. He never stopped loving me. He persevered.

"I will focus on the children," I declared, and I am.

My Sandbox Sidekick

Jan Coleman

What could I say to my friend now? How could I keep from just blubbering all over the place when I saw her lying in a hospital bed in her living room? She was the sister I never had, and in a few weeks a brain tumor would end her life. As I pulled into her driveway, I remembered our childhood, growing up together on a sleepy, suburban street in the San Francisco Bay area. I thought of our first photo I call the "sandbox side-kicks"—me in a messy T-shirt, sporting an impish grin, and Lynne in a ruffled romper, poised for the camera as if she knew that pictures survive long after we do.

Together we conquered skinned knees, bruised bottoms, and baby fat. It became tradition for me to scurry up to her house to confess my current crisis. Be it bookwork or boys, Lynne was always at hand to dissect the day's dilemma. With her customary chuckle and her here-we-go-again sigh, she'd fling open the refrigerator, toss me a crisp green Pippin apple, and the pow-wow would begin.

Her approach was always the same. "Calm down, and we'll look at this thing logically."

When I learned to drive, Lynne was my navigator. When my crush on a high-school quarterback I'd met on summer vacation spurred me to follow his team to games a hundred miles away, Lynne tagged along to keep me in the safety zone. Zipping along country roads with the radio blasting, I would laugh when Lynne said, "My, how you love to live on the edge."

When Lynne left for the university, I received clear directives. "Buckle down and study, and we'll be room-mates next year." Without her as my copilot, my ship sailed off course. When she came home for summer break, I told her of my designs on a handsome young Army man. Three hours and four Pippins later she could not convince me that I was being too hasty, that there is no substitute for time in a dating relationship, and that the deepest needs of my heart could not be met by another person. This time even Lynne could not foil my crusade to mold a private first class into the man of my marriage fantasies.

Fortunately, my friend couldn't see my blushing face when I phoned her fifteen years later with, "He left me and the girls for somebody else." I had other friends to comfort me, but from Lynne I would get a double dose of the prescription most needed. "Find yourself a Pippin," she said, "and let's discuss your options."

When I discovered Lynne had little time left, I cried for the chapter in her life that was ending, for her hopes not yet realized, for her husband, and for her young daughters who would grow up without her. I also cried for myself because I assumed she'd be always there as a fortress in my life and that we would drift into old age together.

Why did I let the busyness of life keep me from nourishing our relationship? We hadn't seen each other for a year when we agreed it was time to "sneak away for the weekend without the kids." I let a problem with my former spouse interfere with our plans, promising her a rain check later on, but we ran out of time.

Lynne wouldn't tolerate living in regret. "It doesn't look good on us," she'd say. So I left my grief at her front door that last day. It was my turn to hold her hand, to brace her with the love and support she had always given me.

We reminisced one last time, laughing over the capers she found herself in trying to protect me. Like the time I insisted on sneaking aboard an aircraft carrier simply because nobody I knew had dared it before.

As our adult years sped by, I often wondered whether Lynne cherished those crazy days because whenever I started to highlight our history for her husband, she'd shoot me a piercing glance.

On our last day together, as we celebrated those memories, I realized those escapades were special to her too. While I needed Lynne's black-and-white logic to keep one foot in reality, she needed to hang out with me to taste life in Technicolor. I spent years longing to be more disciplined and sensible like her, and yet it was my brazen courage and sense of adventure that led her on roads she'd never have explored alone. God teamed us up perfectly.

It's been ten years now, and whenever I face a difficult time, I miss her, but when I start throwing a pity party, I remember our last farewell and my best friend's brave exit from this life. She didn't spend precious energy asking why or blaming God for her circumstances. Lynne did what she always encouraged me to do—confront the truth, accept it, and then take action.

Lynne is waiting for me in heaven. In our first gab session, I'll tell her how her strength and faith inspired me and how I learned from her a principle of God, that hardships become blessings when viewed from the right perspective. I can see Lynne now sitting quietly on a cloud, polishing that plump, green Pippin, ready to toss it to me when I get there.

We Gather Together

Jennifer B. Jones

Mom was waiting for me in the kitchen. She was pretending to write the grocery list for Thanksgiving dinner but was really waiting to tell me the news. I stomped
the snow off my boots and eyed her cautiously.

"Wayne MacBride called," she said. "MacB died
this morning. Wayne was with her and said she went
peacefully."

"Of course he was with her. He took her to Texas
so he could be with her." I practically spat the words,
thinking of the kindly old woman who'd been my
neighbor and friend.

"Laurie, Honey, I know you're hurting," Mom said.
"But this isn't Wayne's fault. He's flying out here next
week to plan her memorial service and to settle her
affairs."

"Which, I assume, means we'll have to move. I
suppose he'll be staying over there." I nodded toward
the half of the house MacB had lived in. "And I suppose you'll be inviting him for Thanksgiving dinner."

"Yes, Laurie. He was her only family. We need to
do something."

"Funny," I said, "I thought we already had."

It was during Thanksgiving dinner the previous
year that MacB had suffered her stroke. She was sitting beside me at the dining room table. One minute
we'd been filling our plates and asking the Lord's
blessing on the incredible meal; the next, MacB was
dropping her fork and staring blankly into space.

We'd stayed at the hospital until she'd been settled in her room in the intensive care unit. When Dad explained to the staff that we were her tenants and her grandson couldn't get a flight in until the next day, they let us see her for a couple of minutes. She'd seemed to have shrunk. Her wrinkled cheeks looked more creased than ever against the crisp white pillowcase.

That night I had hardly slept and prayed more than I had in all my sixteen years. I'd thanked God that she was alive; I'd begged him not to take her away from me.

Wayne had arrived the following day. We'd picked him up from the airport. Dad filled him in on the situation, told him she had seemed completely normal before dinner and had even made her cranberry bread that morning. The emergency squad had responded within minutes. Since the stroke, however, she hadn't moved or spoken.

"Thank you for taking such good care of my grandmother," Wayne said.

"My grandmother," he had said, and I resented the way it sounded, as if she were his possession. His grandmother, not mine.

"Is MacB my grandma?" I had once asked my mother when I was very small. Mom's laughter confused and embarrassed me.

"No," Mom had said, "she's just a wonderful friend."

"Why then," I demanded, wounded, "do we call her MacB?"

"That is short for MacBride, her last name," my mother replied, as if that explained the confusion of human relationships to me.

Sitting beside me on that trip from the airport was the only person who could call her Grandma.

Wayne had stayed for several days in MacB's half of the two-family house we'd lived in my entire life. He spent most of the time at the hospital. When he flew back to Texas, MacB was no closer to returning home than when he'd come to check on her.

After school, I came home to an empty house now. MacB had always been my companion until Mom and Dad came home from work. Dad had kept up the maintenance on the yard and house, and MacB had maintained the people inside it. MacB always insisted she was getting the best end of the bargain.

"Why, if I didn't have you folks," MacB had said, "I'd probably be in some nursing home out in Texas!"

MacB usually saw Wayne once a year. He was only ten years older than me, but those ten years meant the difference between being a kid and being an adult. I didn't mind sharing her with Wayne during those annual visits because it was to me, it seemed, to whom she belonged.

She was the one who went to kindergarten with me on Grandparents' Day, she who attended all my school concerts, she who made my dress for confirmation. It was with us that she celebrated her eightieth birthday. It was at our dining room table that we shared Thanksgiving dinner with her.

Just before Christmas last year, MacB had been moved from the ICU to a regular hospital room. The nurses propped her in a chair for part of every day, but she still could not, or would not, speak.

By spring, I'd thought, *she'll be home by then.*

I watered her African violets and kept the door between our two apartments open at all times, enabling her cat, Clover, to wander freely back and forth.

At the hospital, I'd fed MacB rice pudding, read her the church newsletter, and confided in her, as I always had. Occasionally she would look at me with cloudy eyes. I'd talked to her cheerfully—trying to penetrate the fog that enveloped her.

"Hey, MacB, smile and give your face a rest!" I'd kid her, repeating the expression she'd always used to make me laugh. But MacB's eyes would flutter closed, and I wasn't even sure she'd heard me talking.

With spring had come the promise of new life and renewed hope. I'd kept up my vigil, figuring if I stayed by her side, MacB wouldn't leave me. Surely she'd be home by summer.

By summer, however, Wayne had made arrangements for MacB to move into a nursing home in Texas. I'd begged my parents to bring her home and assured them I could care for her. But Wayne was her family. The decision was his.

The dreaded day of her departure arrived. I'd gone to the hospital to say good-bye. As I'd leaned over to kiss her crinkled cheek, she spoke for the first time in eight months. Her voice, hoarse from disuse, had cracked with emotion. "I can't tell you how much I'll miss you," she said.

She never spoke again.

Wayne had called every week to keep us informed of her condition. His call about her death came as no great surprise. I didn't go to the airport with my parents to pick Wayne up this time. I wasn't sure how I would react to him.

The following day, the day before Thanksgiving, I was off from school. I lingered in bed listening to the shower running and the soft, hurried footsteps on the stairs as my mom and dad got ready for work. Finally, I felt the sudden stir of air through the house as the back door popped shut. Silence.

I knew Wayne had an appointment with the lawyer. I had the house to myself. This was the anniversary of my last normal day with MacB. I lay in bed and held her memory close.

When I realized Clover wasn't in my room begging for her breakfast, I checked downstairs to make sure Wayne hadn't closed the door between the two apartments. But I felt like an intruder the moment I walked through the doorway. The scent of Wayne's aftershave hung in the air, mingling with the fragrance of MacB that still drifted from all that had been hers. I wanted to open a window despite the November chill.

A quick scan of the kitchen explained why Clover hadn't been over to eat—a saucer of milk sat on the floor next to an open bag of Kitty Krunchies.

I walked into the living room, expecting to see Clover curled up on her ledge in the bay window. What I didn't expect was to see Wayne sitting on the couch in the living room, photo albums spread on the coffee table in front of him.

"Come on in," he called, obviously not as startled by my presence as I was of his. The cat stretched out beside him.

"Just so I know in advance, are you moving Clover to Texas so you can take care of her?" I demanded.

He looked puzzled; then a grin started in his eyes and spread over his whole face. "I'm allergic to cats," he said.

"Pity you aren't allergic to people." It seemed much too warm for the sweater I was wearing. I could feel an itchy sweat starting at the back of my neck. I knew I should apologize, but I was afraid great sobs would come out with the words.

"I loved her too," he said.

"You didn't even know her," I told him.

"Not as well as you," he said softly. "Come on." He patted the couch cushion beside him. "Look through her albums with me. I don't know half of these people. You can tell me what you remember about them."

"I remember everything," I said.

There were pictures of me on every page and pictures of MacB with me at every important event in her life and mine. I told him story after story. I hadn't talked this much since July. Every so often we'd come to a page of Wayne pictures, marking MacB's yearly trips to Texas.

The pictures, the stories, the memories—I knew them all by heart. Wayne hadn't taken MacB away from me. I could hold on to the memories forever.

I began to feel comfortable with this man who, now that I was getting to know him, reminded me a lot of his grandmother.

"Wayne?" I asked. "Do you think my family could buy this house?"

"No, Laurie, you can't." My whole body stiffened as if he'd slapped me. If Wayne noticed, he didn't let on.

"After all you have always done for her, it was Grandma's wish that the house belong to the three of you. It's in her will."

"We don't have to move?" I asked dumbly.

"Not unless you want to." Wayne's smile was big and crinkly.

What enormous ears, I thought, *just like MacB.*

"Can you keep a secret?" he asked. "I thought it might be nice to announce the news to your folks during Thanksgiving dinner."

I nodded. I didn't trust my voice.

"Mind if I bring cranberry bread? Of course, you'll have to show me where Grandma kept her recipes."

Again, I nodded.

We sat in silence a few minutes. "Wayne," I said at last, "I can't tell you how much I'm going to miss your grandmother. Or how thankful I am that she was part of my life."

Wayne nodded. I guess he couldn't trust his voice either.

I Want That One

Charles Stanley

I heard a story once about a farmer who had some puppies for sale. He made a sign advertising the pups and nailed it to a post on the edge of his yard. As he was nailing the sign to the post, he felt a tug on his overalls. He looked down to see a little boy with a big grin and something in his hand.

"Mister," he said, "I want to buy one of your new puppies."

"Well," said the farmer, "these puppies come from fine parents and cost a good deal."

The boy dropped his head for a moment, then looked back up at the farmer and said, "I've got thirty-nine cents. Is that enough to take a look?"

"Sure," said the farmer, and with that he whistled and called out, "Dolly. Here, Dolly." Out from the dog-house and down the ramp came Dolly, followed by four little balls of fur.

The little boy's eyes danced with delight.

Then out from the doghouse peeked another little ball; this one noticeably smaller. Down the ramp it slid and began hobbling in an unrewarded attempt to catch up with the others. The pup was clearly the runt of the litter.

The little boy pressed his face to the fence and cried out, "I want that one!" pointing to the runt.

The farmer knelt down and said, "Son, you don't want that puppy. He will never be able to run and play with you the way you would like."

With that the boy reached down and slowly pulled up one leg of his trousers. In doing so he revealed a steel brace running down both sides of his leg and attached to a specially made shoe. Looking up at the farmer, he said, "You see, sir, I don't run too well myself, and he will need someone who understands."

8
Romancing Love

Some pray to marry the man they love,
My prayer will somewhat vary:
I humbly pray to Heaven above
That I love the man I marry.

Rose Pastor Stokes—My Prayer

Love in a Vacuum

Ken Davis

I was settled so deep into my overstuffed armchair that I would have to plan ahead to get out. This was my turf. I deserved this chair, this newspaper, these lazy moments.

Looking up from my crossword puzzle, I saw the door to the storage closet was slightly ajar. Standing in the dim interior was the vacuum cleaner.

I recalled the day I bought the stupid thing. The salesman thought he had died and gone to heaven because it takes very little pressure to sell me. (One time I bought a magnesium fire starter that ignites a campfire in a hurricane, and another time I bought a hand-cranked vegetable compactor that made peanut butter out of recycled zucchini skins.) I salivated as he showed me how the powerful suction of his vacuum cleaner ripped a newspaper to shreds.

I weakened as he leaned closer and lowered his voice. "You won't believe this," he said as he reconfigured the machine to blow air out rather than sucking it in. He held the nozzle of the hose straight upward and placed a Ping-Pong ball in the column of air that now blew from the vacuum cleaner. It bounced up and down, suspended in the column of air. I couldn't even speak.

Then he said, "Watch this!" From his case he pulled a golf ball, placed it in the stream of air, and released it. It fell almost to the nozzle of the hose before it began to bounce and bob in the column of air.

"Other vacuum cleaners won't do a golf ball!" he confided in me. I was already reaching for my wallet.

I paid more than three hundred dollars for that vacuum cleaner, but it never did suck dirt according to my wife. I hadn't touched the thing since I bought it except to demonstrate the Ping-Pong ball trick to visiting friends. In fact, I had not touched many house-cleaning appliances in our marriage. My wife did all that.

You can call me a recovering jerk. For the first fifteen years of our marriage, I did not help Diane make our house a home. Lazy and selfish, I had determined that housework was a woman's work. Diane held down a full-time job to help make ends meet. Additionally, she was my personal secretary and mom to our two daughters. She also waited on me hand and foot and never demanded that I help her.

I really loved my wife, but I had not learned how to show my love. Like a caveman, I made brutish sexual advances, believing that was how a real man expressed love. No wonder our love life had cooled. Oaf that I was, I couldn't figure out the problem with her. Wasn't she grateful? Of all the women I could have married, I chose her.

Now, God was ready to use a vacuum cleaner to teach me a lesson. I stared at the rug-sucker from my armchair and decided to give it a spin. Sure enough, the machine would not pick up important things like toothpicks or burrs. It would fling rubber bands across the room, and it would hold lint for an indiscriminate period of time before spitting it back out.

So I gave up, took the hose off the machine, left it in the middle of the room, and brought stuff to it. The trash I fed it was snatched from my fingers, disappearing into the bowels of the hissing monster. When I could find no more visible trash, I reattached the hose and vacuumed in earnest.

That's when I discovered the stripes. As I vacuumed in one direction, a stripe would appear. Going the opposite direction would create a stripe of a different shade. Fascinated, I striped the whole room. Then I went crosswise, creating a checkerboard pattern. I got so carried away that I dusted the furniture, waxed, and straightened the entire house.

I was reunited with my easy chair when Diane came home. She struggled through the door clutching a bag of groceries under each arm, kicked the door shut with one foot, and then saw the house. Her mouth dropped open. The bags slipped from her grasp and dropped to the floor. "Who did this?" she gasped.

"I did," I said. Then she attacked me.

Diving on me before I could stand up, she smothered me with kisses and thanked me over and over. The kisses grew more passionate. We broke the chair. It was wonderful!

The vacuum cleaner taught me a lesson that day. Love is more than just words. When a husband shares the burdens of homemaking, it shouts "I love you" to any woman. After thirty years of marriage, I still have a lot to learn, but I could never treat my wife again as I did back then.

Now I say "I love you" with a variety of actions. An unexpected card or a bouquet of flowers, picking up after myself, cooking, squeezing toothpaste from the bottom of the tube—all these things bring pleasure to my wife. And the physical passion has returned to our marriage with an intensity that I have not experienced in years.

I've learned my lesson. I keep a Dust Buster with me everywhere we go!

A Legend of Love

LeAnn Thieman

Edward Wellman bade good-bye to his family in the old country and headed for a better life in America. Papa handed him the family's savings hidden in a leather satchel. "Times are desperate here," he said, hugging his son good-bye. "You are our hope." Edward boarded the Atlantic freighter offering free transport to young men willing to shovel coal for its month-long journey. If he struck gold in the Colorado Rockies, the rest of the family could eventually join him.

For months Edward worked his claim tirelessly, and the small vein of gold provided a moderate but steady income. At the end of each day, as he walked through the door of his two-room cabin, he yearned for the woman he loved to greet him. Leaving Ingrid behind before he could officially court her had been his only regret in accepting this American adventure. Their families had been friends for years, and for as long as Edward could remember, he had secretly hoped to make Ingrid his wife. Her long flowing hair and radiant smile made her the most beautiful of the Henderson sisters. He had just begun sitting by her at church picnics and making up silly reasons to stop by her house, just so he could see her. As he went to sleep in his cabin each night, he longed to stroke her auburn hair and hold her in his arms. Finally, he wrote to Papa and asked him to help make this dream come true.

After nearly a year, a telegraph came with a plan to make his life complete. Mr. Henderson had agreed to send his daughter to Edward in America. Because she was a hard-working young woman with a good mind for business, she would work alongside Edward for a year to help the mining business grow. By then both families could afford to come to America for their wedding.

Edward's heart soared with joy as he spent the next month trying to make the cabin into a home. He bought a cot for him to sleep on in the living area and tried to make his former bedroom suitable for a woman. Floral cloth from flour sacks replaced the burlap-bag curtains covering the grimy window. He arranged dried sage from the meadow into a tin-can vase on the nightstand.

At last, the day Edward had been waiting for his whole life arrived. With a bouquet of fresh-picked daisies in hand, he left for the train depot. Steam billowed and wheels screeched as the train crawled to a stop. Edward scanned every window looking for Ingrid's glowing hair and smile.

His heart beat with eager anticipation, then stopped with a sinking thud. Not Ingrid, but her older sister Marta, stepped down from the train. She stood shyly before him, her eyes cast down.

Edward only stared—dumbfounded. Then with shaking hands he offered Marta the bouquet. "Welcome," he whispered, his eyes burning. A smile stretched across her plain face.

"I was pleased when Papa said you sent for me," Marta said looking into his eyes briefly before dropping her head again.

"I'll get your bags," Edward said with a fake smile. Together they headed for the buggy.

Mr. Henderson and Papa were right. Marta did have a great grasp of business. While Edward worked the mine, she worked the office. From her makeshift desk in one corner of the living area, she kept detailed records of all claim activity. Within six months, their assets doubled.

Her delicious meals and quiet smile graced the cabin with a wonderful woman's touch. "But the wrong woman," Edward mourned as he collapsed onto his cot each night. Why did they send Marta? Would he ever see Ingrid again? Was his lifelong dream to have her as his wife to be forsaken?

For a year Marta and Edward worked and played and laughed. Once Marta had kissed Edward on the cheek before retiring to her room. He only smiled awkwardly. From then on she seemed content with their exhilarating hikes in the mountains and long talks on the porch after suppers.

One spring afternoon, torrential rains washed down the hillside, eroding the entrance to their mine. Furiously, Edward filled sandbags and stacked them in the water's path. Soaked and exhausted, his frantic efforts seemed futile. Suddenly Marta was at his side, holding the next burlap bag open. Edward shoveled sand inside, then with the strength of any man, Marta hurled it onto the pile and opened another bag. For hours they worked, knee deep in mud, until the rains diminished. Hand in hand they walked back to the cabin. Over warm soup Edward sighed, "I never could have saved the mine without you. Thank you, Marta."

"You're welcome," she answered with her usual smile, then went quietly to her room.

A few days later a telegraph came announcing the arrival of the Henderson and Wellman families the next week. As much as he tried to stifle it, the thought of seeing Ingrid again started Edward's heart beating in the old familiar way.

Together, Edward and Marta went to the train station. They watched as their families exited the train at the far end of the platform. When Ingrid appeared, Marta turned to Edward. "Go to her," she said.

Astonished, Edward stammered, "What do you mean?"

"Edward, I have always known I was not the Henderson girl you intended to send for. I had watched you flirt with Ingrid at the church picnics." She nodded toward her sister who was descending the train steps. "I know it is she, not me, you desire for your wife."

"But . . ."

Marta placed her fingers over his lips. "Shhh," she hushed him. "I do love you, Edward. I always have. And because of that, all I really want is your happiness. Go to her!"

Edward took her hand from his face and held it. As she gazed up at him, he saw for the first time how very beautiful she was. He recalled their walks in the meadows, their quiet evenings before the fire, her working beside him with the sandbags. It was then he realized what he had known for months.

"No, Marta. It is you I want." Sweeping her into his arms, he kissed her with all the love bursting inside him. Their families gathered around them chorusing, "We are here for the wedding!"

A Matter of Course

Carol McAdoo Rehme

Morning sun clearly defined the mountains, promising a pristine day and beckoning him to answer the call of the links. He had left the house early but not too early, not before helping Mary through their daily routine.

L. K. wiped the dimpled ball, nestled it on the green of the ninth hole, and picked up his marker—not before gently lifting her in and out of the bathtub; not before shepherding her back to the bedroom; not before erasing the ravages of another sleepless night by combing her hair into place.

L. K. gazed at the lush grass as he bent his knees and gripped the putter.

Mary would love walking the course, listening to the hushed stillness. He could point out the geese gliding on the pond and the fragrant crabapple trees laced with blossoms. A love of the outdoors—that was something they shared.

And they shared a lot—six daughters, twenty grandchildren, allegiance to church, devotion to each other. That hadn't changed, but other things had.

L. K. lowered his head and hunched his broad shoulders over the extra-long club.

Once, she agilely whirled with him on the dance floor. Now, the only spinning she did was a turn through the mall in her wheelchair.

Once, her nimble fingers flew at the sewing machine, tucked a blanket around a slumbering child, and tidied the house. Now, crooked and gnarled, they sat—idle in her lap.

L. K. stiffened his wrists.

Rheumatoid arthritis joined their union only nine years into their marriage. He had watched it ravage his wife's body. The changes it made were both immediate and gradual, until—quite clearly—the disease determined their course in life.

L. K. closed his stance and shifted his weight forward.

Some people thought he carried quite a load. But as Mary was able to do less, he simply did more. He merely broadened his definition of *husband,* the job title he considered most sacred. He added the roles of cook, housekeeper, beautician, and chauffeur, even nurse.

He and Mary were good together. After all, they had perfected their teamwork through twenty-four surgeries. He knew better than any health-care worker how to lift her, turn her, and tend to her personal needs. That last hip replacement came at a high price for them both: a permanent infection that added a new element to their routine. Now his large hands tenderly applied fresh dressings twice daily to the draining wound.

L. K. drew the putter into a slow backward stroke.

He rarely glanced back at their old dreams. Instead, together they forged new ones—like purchasing a self-contained motor home so he could assist her in the bathroom, something just not acceptable in public restrooms.

L. K. watched the ball roll forward in a gentle arc and rim the cup. He listened to its satisfying drop and thonk. He made par.

Mary always said other men would have left long ago. She even called him "her good-hearted man." But he liked to remind her that those wedding vows forty-five years past were sincere and binding.

L. K. leaned down and, with his thick fingers, plucked up the ball, brushed it on his pants, and tucked it into his pocket.

There would be other days to golf. It was time to go home. Time to fix lunch. Time to help Mary.

A Wife Gives Thanks

Nancy Hoag

Critically, I watched my husband as he stood inside the main entrance in his red usher's jacket, greeting people, passing out bulletins, and welcoming newcomers to our church. *How I wish he wouldn't wear that old tie,* I thought. And, *why had he gotten his hair cut that short?* Now, our pastor was calling the ushers to the altar. Four were coming forward, one was not. The "one" was my husband. He was fumbling under a seat for the basket he'd put down while talking to a new family who'd wandered in. "For heaven's sake," I began to murmur as I watched my spouse hastily retrieve the basket, stretch his long legs, and catch up with the others.

Watching him with the same impatience I'd felt so often lately, I considered how many times I'd wished he were different. If only he enjoyed traveling. Why couldn't he learn to swim? Why hadn't he been promoted so we could get that transfer back home?

"Honestly! Why doesn't he get with it?" I muttered under my breath. Immediately I "heard" God speak to me.

Read Job 14:3, he said.

"Lord," I replied, "how about if I look it up at home? Our pastor is speaking and getting ready to lead us in prayer."

The thought was there again. *Read Job 14:3 now.*

Anxious to get back to the pastor's teaching for the morning, I grabbed my Bible and began flipping the pages. I located the Scripture passage, put my finger under the verse, and read, "Must you be so harsh with frail men, and demand an accounting from them?" (TLB)

Harsh with frail men? Tears filled my eyes. I glanced up toward the altar as our pastor began reading. Then, turning my head, I looked again at my husband ambling back up the aisle with those long, slow strides of his. Except for my pounding heart, everything in me became still. Although the pastor was just introducing his sermon, God had gotten my attention with private instruction meant for just me.

As my spouse slipped into the pew and hugged my hand, my heart cried out, *Father, forgive my silent sins against my husband. He didn't hear me, but you did. Thank you for helping me see what I was doing. Thank you for this man beside me.*

"Father, thank you for the love this man shows when, with his lunch pail, he sets out for the bus stop each day, even before the sun has risen. Thank you for the care he gives the dog I hauled home from the pound. Thank you for all the hours he's spent with me at flea markets, loaded down with all the 'good deals' I've been unable to resist—and for the times he's escorted me to plays and baseball games, just because I love the theater and hot dogs at the park."

Thank you for shared picnics beside a mountain stream and hikes in the moonlight to glimpse a herd of elk grazing in summer grass. Thank you, Lord, for this unique man—quiet, patient, dependable. Most of all, thank you for letting me see in him a small reflection of the unconditional, protective love you have for us.

I turned to look at my husband again. "Amen," I said, smiling. "Amen."

The Rosebush

Kathy Collard Miller

"Honey, remember that rosebush your mother gave me for Mother's Day?"

Larry stared at me with a look that let me know he really didn't.

"It's been sitting in its pot on the front porch for a month now. I asked you to plant it for me after I got it."

"Oh, yeah, that. Um, let's see. Maybe I could plant it this Saturday." Larry turned back his attention to the baseball game on TV.

Trying not to let hurt and anger overwhelm me, I went through my typical inner conversation: *If he really loved me, that rosebush would have been planted right away. He's in charge of the yard. It's his job.*

Several Saturdays passed, and the rosebush continued to sit in its pot. The longer the rosebush sat on the front porch, the more convinced I was that Larry didn't love me. *It's his responsibility, not mine. I don't know how to plant a rosebush, and I don't especially want to learn. If I do, I'll always have to do it, and it should be his job.*

Several more months passed, and when I stopped to look at it closely one day, I discovered it was dead. "Oh, no, my rosebush!" I cried out.

Staring at the cracked dirt in the pot, I noticed its main root coming up through the dirt. Evidently, it had grown down to the bottom of the pot, and not being able to go down any farther, it grew back up, and about the time it touched the top of the soil, it died.

I felt sad and angry. *Why hadn't Larry planted my rosebush? He makes me so mad. I can't depend upon him for anything, not even planting a rosebush.*

The dead plant seemed to represent Larry's lack of complete love and dedication within our marriage.

I admit now that I could have planted the rosebush and given up my bitterness. But my low self-esteem continually searched for evidence of whether Larry actually loved me. My distrust of his love prevented me from seeing the truth: whether a rosebush got planted had little to do with Larry's level of love and commitment. Now, many years later, I don't judge Larry's love by whether he considers important what is important to me. After all, I don't always consider important what is important to him!

Our love for each other can be unconditional and that's the best way to be!

A Chance of a Lifetime

by Michelle Wolins as told to LeAnn Thieman

"This is a chance of a lifetime," I declared to my friend Stacy as I locked the door of my office and left the restaurant I managed. "It's every twenty-seven-year-old woman's dream to live in New York City, and in a few months I'll know if I get the transfer."

I watched the moonlight glisten on the waters of Laguna Beach. "I'd miss it here, but living in the Big Apple is everything I've ever wanted—a dream come true."

We met a group of our friends at a local café, and I jabbered on about the possibility of my move. Laughter erupted from a nearby table. I watched as a handsome man captured the attention of his friends with his engaging story. His broad, warm smile and air of confidence held me in a trance.

Stacy nudged me. "You're staring, Michelle, and about to drool."

"Wow," I whispered. I watched the gorgeous guy push up the sleeves of his bulky sweater. Everyone at his table had their eyes fixed on him. "That's the man I want to marry."

"Yeah, right," Stacy droned. "Tell us more about where you'll live in New York because we all plan to visit you there when you land this job."

As I spoke, my eyes drifted back to the debonair man.

Three months later my friends and I gathered at

the same restaurant. "To live in the Big Apple!" they cheered as we clapped our glasses together.

"My chance of a lifetime." We talked for hours. I told them of my plan to save money by moving out of my beach cottage and renting a room for the few remaining months.

One friend offered, "I have a fellow South-African friend who is considering renting one of four bedrooms in his house. His name is Barry. A great guy." He scribbled on a napkin. "This is his number. He is a forty-two-year-old confirmed bachelor. Says he's much too busy being a single dad to be a husband."

Later, I made an appointment to see the room. When I approached the entrance of the spacious house, the door opened. "You must be Michelle," the man said. He pushed up the sleeves of his bulky sweater and flashed his handsome smile. It was the man from the restaurant months before—the man I wanted to marry.

I stood staring, my mouth gaping, hoping I wasn't drooling.

"You are Michelle, aren't you?" he said, coaxing me out of my trance. "Would you like to see the room?"

I followed him through a tour of the house, then accepted when he offered me a cup of tea. Barry had a sophisticated kindness about him and listened attentively as I chattered nervously about myself. His silver-rimmed glasses accented a few silver streaks in his dark hair. Soon, his warm, inviting smile put me at ease, and we spent the next two hours talking casually. Ultimately, I decided not to take the room and reluctantly bade him good-bye.

The months went by quickly while I busied myself with preparation for the move. I thought of Barry often, but I couldn't consider calling him.

"I'm moving to New York in two weeks," I said to Stacy as we walked out of my office and into the dining area. "As much as I'd like to see him again, it would only complicate my life."

"Well, brace yourself for complications," Stacy muttered, then nodded toward the door. Barry, with his big blue eyes and engaging smile, walked into my restaurant!

"Hello," he said softly. "Do you have time to join me for a cup of coffee?"

"Of course." I tried not to gasp.

We slid into a booth, and our conversation picked up where it left off before. He, too, was making a career change and was moving back to South Africa. His departure date was one week before mine. Now I knew I had to calm my pounding heart. We obviously had no future together. He took my phone number and invited me to dinner sometime. I accepted, suppressing my sadness, knowing I would be leaving in two short weeks and the date would probably never happen.

But it did. He picked me up a few days later for a movie and dinner. We talked for hours about our lives, our hopes, our separate dreams—mine in New York, his in South Africa. Never had I spoken so freely, so comfortably, with a man. He reached across the table and took my hand. I thought I saw in his eyes the same love I felt swelling in my heart. He said, "I'm just sorry I met you one week before I leave."

"We still have seven days," I said meekly.

"Then let's make the most of it." Hand in hand we strolled to the car and made plans for the next day and the next and the next.

We spent part of every day together for the next week. I knew I was falling in love but dared not speak it. I couldn't upset our chances of a lifetime.

"And I know he loves me too," I moaned to Stacy over a cup of coffee in my near-empty restaurant. "We've even talked about trying to get together over the holidays. He's meeting me here soon to bring me a gift to remember him by."

Just then, Barry strolled in. I stood to welcome his arms around me. We sat, sipping our coffee. "I will miss you so much," he said softly. "But I know you'll think of me whenever you hear this." He placed a Tracy Chapman CD on the table in front of me. Then he pointed to the song title, "Give Me One Reason to Stay Here and I'll Turn Right Back Around," and said, "We can listen to the same music and remember each other."

I gulped my coffee to wash away the lump in my throat. "I'll never forget you, Barry, ever."

"Oh, and one more thing to remember me by." He set a small box on top of the CD. The same awe I felt at our first meeting paralyzed me now. The love I saw in his eyes as we gazed across the table was gift enough for a lifetime. I reached for the box and opened it slowly.

A diamond ring!

"Michelle, I have loved you from the first moment I saw you. On our first date, even before we first had coffee, I knew you were the woman I was going to marry.

"I woke up this morning, desperate, thinking, *It's May third! In three days I'll lose my angel.* Sure, my career in South Africa is a chance of a lifetime, but *you,* Michelle, are my dream come true. Please marry me."

"Yes, Barry, yes," I cried.

"I know what moving to New York means to you, but will you come with me to South Africa?"

"Of course!" I smiled through tears. "You are my chance of a lifetime."

9
God's Love

The light of God surrounds me,
The love of God enfolds me,
The power of God protects me,
The presence of God watches over me,
Wherever I am, God is.

Prayer Card

Getting Carried Away

Linda Evans Shepherd

As a brave mother, I often dragged my young son to places other moms and tots never ventured without strollers with seatbelts.

By the time Jimmy turned three, however, strollers were no longer an option. My active toddler could too easily snap open his seat-belt buckle, then slip away when my nose was buried in a shopping display.

Still, with his small hand in mine, Jimmy and I often braved the world of shopping malls. One day, I boldly walked little Jimmy to the food court to meet his dad for a Chinese dinner at a small orange table. After dinner with a wiggly tot, Paul and I indulged in a little window shopping with Jimmy in tow. Surprisingly, Jimmy did well, not even "losing his cool" when we passed by his favorite ice cream shop.

At 8:30, Paul and I decided to head for home. Paul left us to walk to his trusty red Bronco while Jimmy and I began the long journey out of the mall to my awaiting snow-dusted van.

As we made our way through Sears, Jimmy suddenly flopped to the white-tiled floor. "I'm tired," he said, grabbing my right snow boot in a finger-locking grasp. "Could you drag me for awhile?"

I tried to pull free of Jimmy's grip as a couple of sales clerks giggled.

"Honey, we're almost to the van," I whispered, looking down at the top of his white-blonde head. "Why don't you walk?"

Jimmy clung to my black boot. "I'm too tired. Drag me, Mom. Please?"

I leaned over him. "I don't think I can drag you, but I can carry you. Would that be OK?"

Jimmy looked up and nodded, and I scooped him into my arms. His blue eyes rolled back into his head, and he relaxed into a sleeping lump of dead weight.

As I carried my sleeping child, I thought about the times I'd thrown myself down at God's feet. "I'm too tired to go on. Drag me," I'd cry.

Yet, God's a good Father. He doesn't want to rake me through the muck. He longs to scoop me into his arms and carry me. And when I let him, I can safely rest, even when I am shopping with an exhausted toddler.

In Control

Carolyn R. Scheidies

Uneasiness usually kept me from falling asleep when our children Chris and Cassie were not home, but that Friday night I was so tired I zonked out. I was fast asleep when—BOOM! An explosion rocked the house.

In my dazed mind, the only thing I could think was that the heater had exploded, yet it hadn't been on since spring. My husband Keith sat straight up in bed, but his mind wasn't quite switched on yet. "Something exploded!" he cried.

The next thing I knew, he yelled at me from down the hall. I hurried toward Keith, staring into the white smoke and debris of what had been the main bathroom.

I heard water running and wondered if the house was on fire. Keith turned off the main water valve while I went to pull on some slacks. From the window, I saw a man hurry by. I also saw a van sticking out perpendicular from the house.

Both Keith and I called 911 at the same time from different phones. Then I called my brother who built the house for us several years earlier. He was over almost as quickly as the police.

It didn't take long to discover that both bathrooms had been decimated. The door to the master bath wouldn't even open. After the shock eased, my heart warmed with gratitude.

I continued to feel gratitude, even though we had to live in three different motels in the next week and a half (because they were all so full). My gratitude continued even after we made it home to be further inconvenienced by a constant barrage of repair men.

Why was I grateful when our house was a wreck? Because the list of blessings started that very night. If the van had hit further to the right, it would have wiped out my computer and home office. Further to the left, by inches, and it would have severed a stud and possibly brought the roof down on Keith and me.

It was a Friday night. The van hit us at 12:30 A.M., Chris and Cassie's usual curfew. They could well have been in the bathroom, but they were at a birthday bowling party, which didn't end until an hour later. Further, that party had been postponed from a month earlier.

My brother Paul, a very busy contractor, was at home and on hand not only to make sure we got pictures, but also to make sure the hole in the house was boarded up that night. He insisted I call my sister-in-law to help out, and since my glasses had been in the bathroom, she read off numbers of motels while I dialed. Right down the list I called. Motel after motel turned us away. It was summer and everything was full. Finally, one manager directed us to a newly opened motel. I called, and at two in the morning we had our room with a single bed. No problem; the kids slept on the floor.

I also learned something new about my brother. In this area, when a homeowner wrangled with the insurance company, Paul was the one who mediated. He knew my insurance agent and got that ball rolling with very little trouble.

This series of seemingly unrelated incidences might seem mere coincidences to some, but the probability of all of them happening at once is staggering. God took care of my children, my family, even my home. Instead of increasing my fear, the accident showed me more clearly than any sermon, that no matter what, God is in control.

Unseasonably Christmas

Roberta Updegraff

"Felíz Navidad!" sixteen-year-old Wes called to our coworkers on the Honduran job site. "Merry Christmas" was the only Spanish this youngest member of our work team knew, but "Christmas" in April? We all laughed—Hondurans and Gringos. This out-of-season greeting had broken the communication barrier between our two groups. And little did I realize how profound these words would become during our two-week work mission in Honduras.

When I accepted the call to go to Central America, I thought we were going to assist with building three houses for families who were homeless due to the flood and landslides caused by Hurricane Mitch that fateful October in 1998. Although I'd seen news clips and heard reports of Mitch pummeling the country with four inches of rain per hour, I could not visualize the devastation caused by fifty feet of raging water.

Our Presbytery teamed up with a cooperative of twenty families from one storm-ravaged neighborhood whose residents had committed themselves to working together until each had a new home.

Only three of us spoke Spanish. Yet, we pastors, nurses, businessmen, and truck drivers all had one thing in common—we had heeded God's call in going to Honduras with able hands and willing spirits.

Our team managed to point and motion our way through those first days. I was one of the interpreters

199

and was responsible for interviewing those who came looking for help. But as I listened to their stories, it became apparent that the work we could accomplish was minuscule in comparison to the need. Poverty-shackled hope had little chance of digging out from under fifty feet of sun-baked flood sediment. My sympathetic "I'm sorrys" seemed totally inadequate to help the survivors, *"Los Damnificados,"* as they called themselves, "The Damaged Ones."

I could only cry with my Honduran sisters as they shared memories of that fearsome night when the hurricane took everything they owned.

During the afternoons I met with children for games, songs, and stories. I'd brought two large rod-arm puppets that the children loved almost as much as they seemed to adore me. *"Sebastién! Chicoletta!"* they cried as I approached our shady spot under the plum tree.

I taught them English with songs like "Head, Shoulders, Knees, and Toes," and "What Are You Wearing?" Their delightful Latino accents lifted my spirit and salved my chafed heart. For that little while each afternoon, I almost forgot our circumstances while I basked in the smiles and laughter of the Honduran children.

Still, my nights were sleepless. I attributed my insomnia to an overtired brain stuck in overdrive conjugating Spanish verbs. Yet, something churned within me. My emotions were whirling into a funnel of anger, and the eye of this hurricane seemed to be the center of my soul.

I longed for someone else to vocalize the feelings I was afraid to probe, but no one seemed brave enough to do so. I felt very alone.

One night, as I sat stewing over a minor disappointment with a group member, my disillusionment began to seep into my conversation. I felt betrayed, yet couldn't bring myself to admit it. Suddenly, I had to flee the dining room before I broke down in front of everyone. As I sobbed under the starless sky, I realized that it was not human betrayal I was struggling with; it was God's.

You could have stopped the rain! I screamed silently. You held back the sea for Moses and the Israelites. Jesus tamed a storm for friends one night on the Sea of Galilee.

A deluge of doubt sent tremors through me as I tried to reconcile the seemingly diametric realities I was experiencing. God was good and kind, always looking out for our best interests; yet these people were his children too. They loved him and had prayed for a miracle that did not come.

Lord, how could you turn your back on these people and their suffering?

My cries were met with silence. But the next morning, things began to change. Geri, a member of our group, sought me out to say she shared the frustration I'd vocalized the previous night. She, too, was weathering an emotional storm.

She confided, "I'm a listener. I've worked most of my life comforting people. I understand grief . . . if only I could communicate."

I sorely wished I had her problem, for I found the pain was in the understanding of their language.

Geri sighed, "Perhaps I'm here not to give but to receive." She smiled ruefully at that explanation. "Maybe God has something to teach me. He's stripped me of my confidence, that's for sure. I feel useless." She smiled again. "Maybe I'm even teachable at this point."

I nodded, but inside I doubted whether God really cared about any of us. He seemed so far away.

I went back to collecting rocks for the house foundation, giving little more than perfunctory answers to my Honduran friends' attempts at conversation. But as I worked, an eerie calm began to envelop me—a shell-shocked calm—and I knew I must face the wreckage in my soul.

"How do you pick up the pieces?" I said to no one in particular. Ledy, a widowed mother of four, met my gaze.

She answered, "I could not."

I stared at her as I struggled with my emotions. She went on, "There was nothing left to pick up."

I started crying and so did she.

"It's so horrible—my heart hurts," I sobbed. "How do you hold on?"

"When the storm was over," she said softly, "God was still there—arms open."

"But he could have stopped the rain," I cried. "Ledy, you lost your husband, your home, everything! Didn't you want to run from God?"

"Where would I go?"

We held each other and she encouraged me.

"Honduras is a poor country, but we are a proud people. We took care of ourselves—until Mitch."

She explained that first she thought the hurricane was divine retribution for their self-centeredness, but as the Honduran Christians clung to one another, she realized that God had simply allowed a storm to teach them something very important. Mitch made them vulnerable. "We may be *'Los Damnificados,'*" she told me. "But we are only broken, not destroyed."

Although she didn't totally understand why the lesson had to be so devastating, she recognized that God hurt with them. "We have hope," she told me.

As I struggled to regain composure, she wiped the tears from my face. "God cares," she whispered. "He sent you to us."

"But what can we accomplish compared to this?" I motioned toward the destruction in the valley below. "It is so little, so very little."

"In love, it is much, very much."

Just then, that now familiar, *"Felíz Navidad!"* rang from behind us as Wes and Ledy's nephew, Carlos, waved from the back of a pickup.

"Felíz Navidad," the other workers at our job site shouted back.

Several little boys scrambled to the truck to join our team in unloading sand for cement, and brilliant grins lit deep-tanned faces. Love spoke with laughter and clinking shovels. Geri caught my eye and smiled.

José, one of the two Honduran pastors, motioned for me to sit in the cab with him so he could show me newspaper accounts of the hurricane. As I voiced my pain and confusion, he shared some of his experiences and sang me a song about hope—of transforming disappointment into joy by working together for one another. *"Que No Caiga La Fe"* ("Don't Give Up the Faith") had become their theme song.

Later that day, when taking my place at the center of my group of children, I felt rejuvenated, perhaps reborn. I'd brought a storybook version of the Gospel, and when I opened it the children exclaimed, *"Jesucristo! Jesucristo!"* clamoring to show me crosses and to share their faith. I sat back and let them read the story to me, their guileless black eyes drawing me in. Together we splashed in puddles of wonder at God's amazing grace.

"Felíz Navidad," whispered the still, small voice to my now calm spirit.

I looked around at the men and women sifting through the destruction. They were the survivors who were trying to rebuild their lives. The storm was over and they were not destroyed. God was here, with arms open, and his love meant much, very much. For they had hope, and now, so did I. For not only did God send me to them, he sent them to me.

Are You God?

Charles R. Swindoll

Shortly after World War II came to a close, Europe began picking up the pieces. Much of the old country had been ravaged by war and was in ruins. Perhaps the saddest sight of all was that of little orphaned children starving in the streets of those war-torn cities.

Early one chilly morning, an American soldier was making his way back to the barracks in London. As he turned the corner in his Jeep, he spotted a little lad with his nose pressed to the window of a pastry shop. Inside, the cook was kneading dough for a fresh batch of doughnuts. The hungry boy stared in silence, watching every move. The soldier pulled his Jeep to the curb, stopped, got out, and walked quietly to where the little boy was standing. Through the steamed-up window, he could see the mouth-watering morsels as they were being pulled from the oven, piping hot. The boy salivated and released a slight groan as he watched the cook place them onto the glass-enclosed counter ever so carefully.

The soldier's heart went out to the nameless orphan as he stood beside him.

"Son . . . would you like some of those?"

The boy was startled.

"Oh, yeah . . . I would!"

The American stepped inside and bought a dozen, put them in his bag, and walked back to where the lad was standing in the foggy cold of the London morning.

He smiled, held out the bag, and said simply, "Here you are."

As he turned to walk away, he felt a tug on his coat. He looked back and heard the child ask quietly: "Mister . . . are you God?"

We are never more like God than when we give.

God so loved the world that he gave.

The Man I Met in the Attic

Bruce Bickel and Stan Jantz

My father died when I was four years old. I grew up never knowing much about him. My mother had remarried a wonderful man who adopted me and loved me. I didn't have a burning desire to find out who my birth father was until a few years ago. My wife, Karin, and I decided to go back to Minnesota to visit the place of my heritage and maybe to find Dad.

I'll never forget the experience. Karin and I stayed with my father's older brother, Sam. As you can guess, it didn't take long for Uncle Sam to ask me if I wanted to see photos of my dad, as well as some of the letters he had written. I quickly agreed.

The three of us climbed into his attic where all the stuff was stored in an old trunk. My uncle pulled the light on with a string. We sat on boxes in that musty attic, passing around fading photos, reading letters aloud, and listening to Uncle Sam tell story after story.

That's how I "met" my father, in that attic where all the stuff was stored in an old trunk.

In that attic, I got a complete picture of the kind of man Dad was and what he did for me. I saw myself in a different light, too, because I discovered that we shared many physical features and personality traits. For the first time I knew what it meant to say, "I am my father's son."

On your search for God, think about my journey to that attic in Minnesota. The Bible is like an old trunk, full of pictures and letters from God (your heavenly Father) to you, someone he loves very much.

10
Love Inspires

Expect people to be better than they are;
it helps them to become better. But don't
be disappointed when they are not;
it helps them to keep trying.

Merry Browne

The Blue of Jimmy's Eyes

Linda Evans Shepherd

December snowflakes swirled outside my window as the radio played familiar Christmas carols in the background. But this festive mood was lost to me. I closed my eyes, imagining my dad in Texas decorating the Christmas tree and happily humming "Jingle Bells." I could see Mom in the kitchen baking her famous fruitcake cookies. I could picture Jimmy, my twenty-two-year-old brother, wrapping Christmas gifts in bright red paper.

A little over a year ago, we feared my brother might not live to see another Christmas after he was hit by a drunk driver. He looked so broken and pale as he lay on the crisp, white sheets in intensive care, hooked to machines and tubes. He could only blink his eyes to communicate.

We stroked his hair and prayed. The doctors had told us, "Even if he lives, he'll be a quadriplegic."

Yet, not only did he live, he learned to use his hands and arms again.

That year, Mom, Dad, and I kidnapped Jimmy from his rehab center for a family Christmas celebration back home in Beaumont. Jimmy proudly sat in his wheelchair, surrounded by our love. We cheered when on Christmas morning he stood and took his first faltering steps. Only a few months later, he amazed his doctors by walking out of the Houston rehab center, totally free of his former paralysis.

It was time to rejoice in Jimmy's victory; only this

Christmas I was not able to make the trip to join the celebration.

I opened my eyes to see the Colorado snowflakes continue their dance across the frozen landscape. A joyful Christmas tune faded as a disc jockey's voice announced, "Christmas, for many, generates feelings of loneliness. To bust those blues, reach out to others."

Great idea, I thought, *only all my friends have already left for their holiday destinations. I pouted. Isn't there anyone who needs me?*

I smiled as I envisioned the sweet-faced grandmothers who lived at the local nursing home. *That's it!* I decided, eagerly making plans to shop for chapstick and hand lotion.

Christmas morning came, and I had second thoughts. Who am I? Some silly Pollyanna?

I stared hard at my basket filled with wrapped trinkets. These gifts were nothing more than cheap drugstore specials. Still, I had to muster my courage and face the grandmothers who awaited me. Besides, I'd do almost anything to keep my mind off what I was missing in Texas.

When I pulled my old yellow Maverick into the nursing home parking lot, I sat shivering in my car and staring at the bleak, snow-dusted building.

I breathed in a lung full of frigid air, then slipped into the cold. I pulled open the nursing home door and stepped into the empty lobby. My heart pounded. Just as I decided to flee, a young blonde nurse appeared behind the front desk. "May I help you?" she asked.

"I'm here to visit someone," I stammered.

"Who?"

"Uh, anyone. I mean, someone who needs a visitor," I replied, feeling foolish.

The nurse appeared thoughtful, then smiled. "I know just the person. Follow me."

Still feeling uncertain, I obeyed. Even our footsteps sounded lonely as we walked down the hall. I glanced in rooms where I saw glum-faced elderly residents. Although their sadness panged me, I was not prepared for my next encounter.

We rounded the corner, and the last images of my vision of hugging sweet grandmothers evaporated. There before me lay the grotesque form of a drooling man slumped in his bed with his limbs drawn into a permanent fetal position.

I tried to hide my shock with a frozen smile as the nurse turned to face me.

"This is Jimmy," she said, "he was injured in a motorcycle accident. I'll leave you two alone so you can visit."

I froze. Did the nurse really say, "Jimmy"?

Trying not to panic, I looked down into Jimmy's lonely thirty-five-year-old twisted face. Paralyzed and brain damaged, he could only communicate by blinking his eyes. Unsure of what to say, I silently prayed, *Lord, now what?*

I tried to introduce myself. "H-hi, I'm L-Linda."

Jimmy blinked his welcome.

"Here," I said, shoving a brightly wrapped tube of chapstick into his withered hand. I then stammered, "M-Merry Christmas!"

I could feel my face flush with shame as I helped him unwrap the gift. *How thoughtless! What would a paralyzed man do with a tube of chapstick?*

Amazed, I realized that he was not laughing at me, nor was he angry.

Encouraged, I began to ask him questions, but I became confused as I tried to decipher his blinked messages.

When Jimmy looked amused at my befuddlement, I couldn't help but smile.

Before I knew it, I was telling him homespun tales and narrating the Christmas story of God's Christmas gift to humankind, a babe born in a manger.

Jimmy's blue eyes twinkled, and I was no longer afraid.

Although this Jimmy was not *my* Jimmy, somehow he seemed like family. As I had done with my brother on that night of tragedy, not so long before, I stroked Jimmy's hair and whispered a prayer. My knees were shaking when I finally left his side.

I spent the rest of the afternoon fulfilling my vision of hugging sweet grandmas. My presence could not have been more appreciated. How glad I was when I checked my loneliness at the nursing home door. By reaching out to others, I had received a greater gift. I had found a Merry Christmas in the blue of Jimmy's eyes.

Best Present of All

Bonnie Compton Hanson

I quickly scanned the rest of my list. This was already Friday night, and because my weekend was going to be so busy, I was trying to finish my grocery shopping as quickly as possible.

What did I still need? Oh, yes, flowers—for we would be visiting my in-laws that weekend for a big dual birthday celebration. Dad was now a young ninety-three; his wife, eighty-three. So after church that Sunday we planned to drive out to their home and take them out for a nice birthday dinner.

After selecting a colorful fall arrangement, I checked my list again. Birthday cards for both of them. Pushing my piled-high cart around to the greeting card aisle, I noticed a young girl there with her mother. It was hard not to. The attractive child was positively glowing with excitement as she held up two gaily colored cards. "Oh, Mom!" she bubbled. "They're both so cool. Can't I get both of them?"

Smiling, the mother shook her head. "No, darling, just one. Hurry and choose the one you want."

"Oh, but I can't choose!" Turning to me, a perfect stranger, she grinned.

"Look—aren't they both just adorable? Which one should I pick?"

I laughed. "Well, dear, that depends on who it's for. Tell me what your friend is like, and I'll give you my recommendation."

She stared at me blankly. "Friend? What friend?"

"Why, the one you're buying the card for, of course."

She giggled. "Oh, my goodness! Didn't you know? The card is for me! See, my birthday's tomorrow. So for my present this year, Mom said I could pick out any card I want all by myself. Isn't that great? OK, Mom, I think I'll take this one." Holding tightly to one card, she put the other one back.

Hardly believing what I'd just heard, I stuttered, "W-why, congratulations, dear! How old will you be?"

Hugging her mother, she said, "Eleven."

Tears sprang to my eyes. How could any child—especially an eleven-year-old—get nothing more for her birthday than a two-dollar card?

It just wasn't fair! My first impulse was to reach right into my purse, grab the ten-dollar bill tucked inside, and thrust it into this poor child's hand. After all, I'd be paying for all my own purchases by check, so I didn't really need the cash. Wouldn't that be a loving thing to do?

Then I looked at the embarrassed mother. She was probably a single mom trying desperately to make ends meet. How it would shame her if I did such a thing! So my purse stayed unopened.

"Happy birthday, dear!" I replied instead.

Mother and daughter beamed at each other. Hugging tightly to each other and to the precious card, they hurried off to the checkout stand—having already given to each other the best and most priceless birthday present in the whole world: the gift of love.

Touching the Untouchable

Naomi Rhode

He was admitted to emergency receiving and placed on the cardiac floor. He had long hair and an unshaven face. He was also dirty and dangerously obese. His black motorcycle jacket was tossed over the bottom shelf of the dresser.

This man was certainly an outsider to this sterile world of shining Terrazzo floors, efficient uniformed professionals, and strict infection-control procedures. *He was an untouchable!*

The nurses at the station looked wide-eyed at this mound of humanity that was wheeled by—each glancing nervously at my friend Bonnie, the head nurse. "Let this one not be mine to admit, to clean, to bathe, to tend to," was their pleading, unspoken message.

Unbelievably, it was Bonnie who said, "I want this patient for myself."

As she donned the latex gloves and proceeded to take this huge, very unclean man to his room, her heart almost broke.

Where was his family? Who was his mother? What was he like as a little boy?

She hummed quietly as she worked. It seemed to ease the fear and embarrassment she knew he must be feeling.

And then on a whim she said, "We don't have time for back rubs in hospitals these days, but I bet one would feel really good. And it would help you to relax your muscles and start to heal. That is what this place is all about, a place to heal."

As she massaged his shoulders, she notice his thick, scaly, ruddy skin, which told her of an abusive lifestyle. *Probably a lot of addictions to food, alcohol, and drugs,* she realized.

As she rubbed those taught muscles, she hummed and prayed. She prayed for the soul of a little boy grown up, rejected by life's rudeness and striving to be accepted in a hard and hostile world. The finale was warmed lotion and baby powder. It was almost laughable, the lotion and powder were such a contrast to this huge, foreign surface.

As he rolled over onto his back, the tears were rolling down his cheek, and his chin trembled. With amazingly beautiful brown eyes, he smiled and said in a quivering voice, "No one has touched me for years. Thank you, I *am* healing."

The challenge for a hurting world is to still dare to touch the untouchable—through eye contact, a warm handshake, a concerned voice—or, as in Bonnie's gift, the physical reassurance of warmed lotion and baby powder.

The Words of a Dummy

Gail Wenos

As a ventriloquist, I see God use my "dummy" Ezra in many different ways. At one of my speaking engagements, I saw a "dummy" cure someone who couldn't talk and another person who felt ugly.

The Plaza in Portland, Oregon, is a graduated care facility. Included in the facility is a convalescent section called the Health Care Center. The lady in charge of the vespers asked if I could spend a few minutes in the center. *No problem,* I figured. *I can easily do a fifteen-minute program.* Well, God had other things in mind.

With about fifteen people there, in all stages of disability—many in wheelchairs and several unable to tell me their names—I realized that a "program" was out of the question. The best thing was to have Ezra visit each individual. What a joy it was to see those dear people respond to Ezra as he stood on their knees and talked to them.

Then we got to Katie, who is a tiny woman. She doesn't have a tooth in her head, but she has the sweetest face. There she sat in her wheelchair, all bundled in pink and holding a small teddy bear.

She was looking down when I approached her. But when I stood Ezra on her knees and he said, "Merry Christmas, Katie. I love you!" Katie lifted her head and her eyes lit up. She gave Ezra the most beautiful toothless grin I've ever seen. Ezra and Katie then began to carry on a rather animated conversation. I was trying to keep my focus on Katie, but I was keenly aware that something was going on with the staff. They were jumping up and down, hugging each other, laughing and crying at the same time. It wasn't until a few minutes later that I found out why. Katie hadn't talked in years! But there she was, talking a blue streak with Ezra.

Then there was Ada—not as sweet-looking as Katie. In fact, with rotting teeth, a slight drool, a whiskery chin, and disheveled hair, Ada actually was a bit homely. She kept bending down to stroke the legs of her chair, or she would pat herself. She, too, was in her own world. But each time Ezra would come to her she would stop the motions, then hold onto Ezra as she smiled and laughed, making her face light up with delight. In her delight, God let me see a special kind of beauty. I'm so grateful he did. As I stood Ezra on her knees, I had no idea that Ezra's simple words of "Ada, you is beautiful!" would have such a tremendous impact.

As soon as Ezra told her she was beautiful, Ada looked at him with stunned disbelief. "I'm beautiful! Oh! Do you really think I'm beautiful?" And when Ezra truthfully responded, "Yes, Ada, you *is real* beautiful. Merry Christmas!" Ada gave him a hug and her tears began to flow. Then she held him back, looked at him with a truly beautiful smile as she said with laughter, "Oh, yes, it is a Merry Christmas. I'm *beautiful*." As far as I was concerned, I had the richest Christmas ever!

The Travelers

Bobbie Wilkinson

I watched as she led him by the hand to the bathroom at the airport terminal. Travelers surrounded them, rushing past, and although he seemed a little bewildered, his security was assured as long as his hand was in hers.

Returning to their seats at the gate, she combed his hair and straightened his tie. He asked a lot of questions about what time it was and when they would get to ride the plane, which was an hour delayed. I marveled at the mother's patience and love and watched her take him by the hand when she was finally allowed to board.

Upon finding my way to my seat, I discovered that the three of us would be together: I, with the window seat, he, the middle, and the mother, the aisle. I told him how handsome he looked in his suit, and he smiled.

She helped him take his jacket off and buckled him into his seatbelt. He said that he had to go to the bathroom again, and she assured him that he could last until the end of the flight. (I quietly hoped she was right!)

As the jet engines were started, he became frightened and reached for her hand. She explained what was going on and began talking to him about their trip. He was confused about the different relatives they would be seeing, but she patiently repeated who was who until he seemed to understand.

He asked many more questions about the time, what day it was, how much longer until they got there . . . and she lovingly held his hand and gave him her full attention.

She and I introduced ourselves and shared the usual things all mothers like to share with one another. I learned she had four children and was on her way to visit one of her daughters and her grandchildren.

The hour passed quickly, and soon we were preparing to land. He became frightened again, and she held his hands tightly in hers and gently stroked his arm reassuringly. He said, "I love you, Mom," and she smiled and hugged him. "You know I love you too."

They got off the plane before I did, the mother never realizing how deeply she had touched me. I said a quiet little prayer for this remarkable woman and for myself—that I would always have enough love and strength to meet whatever challenge came my way, as this extraordinary mother clearly had. She will never stop being a mom, you see, because her companion was a child who had come unexpectedly and very late in her life—her beloved husband of more than forty years, who now has Alzheimer's.

When I last saw them, she was holding his hand as she led him to the baggage claim area at the airport. "God bless this mother," I said to myself. "God bless *all* mothers."

Miss Lillian

Steve Wise

I was six years old when I saw her for the first time, eighteen when I saw her for the final time, and during the twelve years that I knew Miss Lillian, she taught me so much about the enduring qualities of life that scarcely a week passes that I do not think of her. I doubt that anyone who ever met Miss Lillian forgot her quickly, if at all.

She was waiting patiently in the first-grade classroom when the ragtag collection of which I was a part trundled into her room on a steamy September morning in 1954. One by one, we stole sidelong glances at the front of the room where she stood smiling pleasantly with her hands folded in front of her. The excited chatter that trailed in from the hallway soon died away, and those of us who had never before seen her fell silent as we attempted not to stare.

The only reason that our teacher stood taller than most of us was that she wore shoes with two-inch heels. Her tiny body was devoid of a neck, with her head resting squarely on narrow shoulders. Her brown hair was immaculately done and framed an adult-sized face with cheery features and prominent cheekbones brushed daintily with rouge. She waited until the last of the stragglers entered the room before she spoke to us in the steady confident tones of one who was accustomed to being stared at and who was unfazed by the piercing eyes of children. I do not remember what she said to us, but I do remember that by the end of that first day Miss Lillian Allen had begun to secure a place in my heart that remains hers to this day.

Within days, we were all snuggled into her nest of care and learning—each assured of his or her great worth, each comforted after any bumps or scrapes suffered on the playground, each loving the sound of her voice as she read to us after lunch. After a month, those of us who had snickered the loudest at the initial sight of her on the first day of class would have fought mightily against anyone who dared slight Miss Lillian.

A couple of years later, I remember the pity I felt when my father first told me of the tragedy that had stricken her. Dropped in infancy on a concrete floor by an older sister, Miss Lillian's spine had been severely damaged and her growth stunted forever. My father saw the pity in my eyes and quickly assured me that it was wasted on a woman who neither desired nor needed it, however genuine the sentiment on my part.

"Forget what she looks like," he advised me, "she's one of the finest women God ever put on this earth." This from a man who meted out praise as carefully as a pharmacist measures a potent medicine.

As I progressed through the grade-school years, Miss Lillian was never far from my thoughts at school. A glimpse across the recess yard, a smile returned as she passed by in the lunch line, a wave from across the street as she walked home—small things all, yet somehow links in a chain that connected us until I was nearly thirteen. That was the age at which my father decided I should begin to earn at least some of my spending money. With his help, I soon acquired several lawn-cutting jobs within a few blocks of our home.

To my delight, Miss Lillian's lawn became my responsibility, and to this day, I do not know if she stopped taking care of the yard herself because she had grown weary of it or if she wanted me to have the job. Whatever the reason, I was determined to make her happy with the decision, and I labored with all the diligence that my thirteen-year-old mind and body could muster. Finally satisfied with my handiwork, I would mop my brow with my shirttail and trudge up the steps to join her on the porch for the three things that were always waiting—pleasant conversation, freshly squeezed lemonade, and two one-dollar bills.

There, on that porch, in the wonderful haze of teenage summers, Miss Lillian planted lasting seeds in my soul, and there I see her when I seek the counsel of her spirit. It was there, when after confiding various worries to her, she said, "Except for other people, if you can touch it with your fingers or see it with your eyes, then it can't be worth worrying about for long." There, the summer after I acquired my first BB rifle, I learned it was a sin to kill a mockingbird. There I learned to think of smiles as priceless gifts to offer to my fellow sojourners in life. The breezy front porch was the place where I was gently admonished to remember that my tongue, oftentimes given to action before thought, could cut hearts like a knife could cut warm bread. She spoke and I listened. She taught and I learned.

The front porch of the little house on Hodge Street was the last place I ever saw her, long after I had outgrown mowing lawns for money and several years after Miss Lillian had retired from teaching. She had grown old far too soon, the tiny, frail body ill-suited to withstand the ravages of time, and for a moment she allowed her weariness to show as I stopped on the sidewalk to say hello. But it passed with the twinkle of her eye, and she offered a smile as a parting gift.

I have two teenaged children now, and although I have confidence that their teachers do their best, I cannot help but lament the fact that my children will never meet someone like Miss Lillian. But I have told them of her. Would to God that I may be able to make her real to them with words both spoken and written.

Ten years ago, my daughter Stacee gave me hope that this desire is being fulfilled. During a quiet talk at bedtime, she wondered aloud why God had not allowed Miss Lillian to have children of her own. Then, before I could formulate a suitably lofty parental answer, Stacee enlightened both of us.

"You were kinda like a kid of hers, Daddy. All of you were. Just think. She must have had a thousand!"

"Yes, girl . . . yes, you're right. Miss Lillian surely must have had a thousand children."

11
Love through Loss

'Tis better to have loved and lost,
Than never to have loved at all.

Tennyson—In Memoriam

The Man Who Gave Me the World

Nancy Bayless

Grandfather opened a world of wonder and strength for a little girl and walked with her to the last door of childhood.

My grandfather had a hard lap, but his arms were gentle as he held me. He always put his knees together so I wouldn't fall through the space between his legs.

He was a retired judge, tall and thin with white hair and skin as pink as a baby's. He wore a monocle on a narrow black grosgrain ribbon, and he had a pocket watch the size of a salad plate. He'd swing the watch on its heavy golden chain and hold it to my ear with infinite patience.

He peeled an apple better than anyone in the whole world. First he would get out his pocket-knife and wipe it on his clean white handkerchief. There was never a speck of dirt on the knife, but he would wipe it anyway.

Then he reached his arms around me as I sat on his lap, and he peeled the apple. The curling red skin trailed down over my body and almost touched the floor. It was magical.

My grandfather shaved with a straight razor, and when we went to visit him, I sat on the edge of the bathtub to watch him shave. While he got out all the things he needed to shave, I slid into the bathtub and pulled myself to the rim again. I counted out loud and usually slid up and down five times before he was ready.

Then I counted while he stropped his razor to get it good and sharp. He always whacked it exactly twenty times before he made some lather by whirling his fluffy brush around in his wooden soap bowl. The wonderful fragrance of Yardley's filled the air, and he dabbed a bit on my nose, swirled some on his face, and got to work.

When he was squeaky clean and completely rinsed off with a steamy hot washcloth, he slapped on Bay Rum aftershave and picked me up so we could admire his glowing face in the mirror.

Every day Grandfather took me for a walk and pointed out to me all the wonders of God. He made me stop and listen to the murmurs of the morning, the voices of each noon, and the whispers of each night.

Our noon walks usually included a juicy hot dog at our favorite stand and a chocolate milkshake so thick we had to eat it with a spoon.

Our night walks were a lesson in astronomy. Sometimes we found clean grass growing on the sides of the city sidewalk, and we stretched out on our backs. We pretended to shine Orion's belt buckle or take an invisible brush and give a hundred strokes to Venus's hair.

My grandfather loved the rain, so we would suit up and splash through puddles and look at reflections in the pools of water when the ripples stopped. If it was spring and we were in the right spot, we would see cherry blossoms and the Washington Monument shimmering in the same pool.

I don't remember receiving gifts from my grandfather, but he gave me the world. And he talked to me about God's love and why I should live by the Ten Commandments.

He'd light his pipe and reach for his Bible while I curled up on a footstool at his feet. He read the same verses over and over until I had them memorized like nursery rhymes. From time to time, he would pause to stroke my hair and explain something to me.

When I was ten years old, my grandfather became ill with cancer, and he stayed in his bed, sometimes letting out groans of agony. His magnificent body wasted away, and they wouldn't let me go into his room because he was too sick.

I knew he could never be too sick to see me. So I stood in his doorway, and when the sun was just right, my shadow fell across his bed and caressed his face.

Once in a while, he reached out to take my shadow hand, and I stood there like a sentry to give him my strength.

One morning, when his nurse was out of the room, he motioned for me to come in. I ran to his bed-side and took his fragile hand in mine. His eyes treasured my face, and he smiled. I couldn't stop the tears.

I spewed out the anguish in my heart and sobbed about how I hated God for letting him get sick. His eyes became stern, and his hand tightened in mine. He spoke in a harsh whisper, "Don't ever hate God, my darling girl. He always knows what he's doing. And though I love you, I want to be with him. Trust him, no matter how much you hurt inside."

"And remember the Ten Commandments," he said, "because you tell lies sometimes, don't you?" His eyes bored into my soul.

I nodded and looked away. I wanted to scream that I never lied to him. Never! Never! Never! But I was sure he wouldn't believe me.

"Always be honest to yourself, Honeybunch," he said, "And always love the Lord." He smiled again, a smile that washed me clean. I wanted to throw myself across him and die for him in his place. He sensed my longing and patted my hand.

"Be strong," he said. "You're a big girl now, and grandmother will need your strength." Then he let go of my hand and turned away from me.

I backed slowly out of the room, one tiny step at a time. Then I ran to the cavernous hall closet and grabbed my wooden hoop and the stick that made it roll. My clown mask was on the shelf, and I put it on to hide my tears.

It was hot outside, and darkness was edging around the day. Large drops of rain splashed on the slate sidewalk, and little wisps of steam were rising around the wet spots. It was slippery and I slid along, furiously striking my hoop and trying not to fall. Grandfather's words branded themselves on my brain, and I thought about some of the Bible verses he had drilled into me.

Suddenly I ripped off my mask and threw it as far as I could. I held my hoop up off the sidewalk and turned back toward the apartment. He was right. Grandmother was going to need my strength, and I must remind her that God always knows what he's doing.

The sanctuary overflowed for my grandfather's service, and there was a traffic jam as people came from far and near. It surprised me that he had so many friends. I thought of him as mine and Grandmother's.

I left my childhood behind that day. I realized for the first time how powerful one person's life can be as it touches other people's lives.

Grandfather inspired me to live the simple truth in the Bible with quiet gentleness and sincerity. I knew this would help his legacy to live on in me.

The Special Date
Carmen Leal-Pock

Ken and Rose celebrated their twenty-sixth anniversary recently. Rose has Huntington's Disease, a terminal neurological disorder, and now resides in a nursing home. Ken took some time off work on their special day to take Rose out for lunch.

When they passed a pizza parlor, she said, "Pizza!" So pizza it was, followed, or should I say, overlaid by ice cream. As they were having their pizza, Rose kept saying, "I love pizza." Normally she says only one word, sometimes two. To string three words together is a real achievement at this point. In the midst of keeping her from burning herself on piping hot pizza, and from choking on the gooey stuff, he paused and held her hands. She looked up and clearly said, "I love you."

It is easy to dream of an anniversary meal served at a fine restaurant on beautiful china with the best service. However, for Ken, nothing shall ever compare to the back seat of their Dodge. Covered in pizza and ice cream and being told by the only person who has ever really mattered to him (not counting his wonderful children) that he was loved, makes life not just bearable, or worth living, but for Ken, it makes life outrageously magnificent!

Ken admits to being, by nature, a sentimental person, perhaps an absolute Pollyanna about most things. He says, "Rose is the sole reason I'm here, the only reason I know how to express love. She stands at the absolute center of my life. Though ill and but a shadow of her former self, her power to love is undiminished. I thank God for his kindness. Happy anniversary, my dearest Rose."

The Vacuum

Suzy Ryan

The vacuum broke, and my heart suddenly felt broken too. Why am I so upset just because my sweeper is on the blink?

I knew why. My eighteen-year-old brother, Bart, had sold me the vacuum six months before he killed himself. As a newlywed, I didn't really have the extra money for the expensive vacuum, but knowing that no one else in the family would buy one from him, I bought it anyway.

Now I couldn't bear to throw it away. Somehow it seemed to symbolize my love for Bart. As I used my sweeper, it relieved my raging thoughts about his death: *Could I have prevented him from committing suicide? Should I have found a psychiatrist and insisted on therapy?*

Although I knew Bart had previously tried to take his own life in the tenth grade, he'd never talked about it. He wouldn't admit that he suffered from manic depression. He would only sporadically take his medication, insisting he was perfectly normal.

At twenty-four, I felt such responsibility for Bart because he depended on me. My two siblings and I all had different fathers, as Mom was on her fourth marriage, so our loyalty to one another remained our security.

Bart's charming personality and chiseled good looks made him appear like a healthy boy. And sometimes he was. At other times he was detached. And though he was bright, witty, and had a tender spirit, he never had any friends. He never made good grades and never experienced success.

Although he pretended to choose to remain home alone, I knew differently. Once, when he was nine, he asked me to call a classmate named Johnny to invite him to a movie. Johnny accepted, and Bart's countenance brightened at the prospect of a friendship. He appeared genuinely content. But when Johnny never called again, I saw Bart's blue eyes darken with rejection. His insecurity and solitary life broke my heart!

Determined to compensate for his suffering, I allowed Bart to live in my shadow. He attended football games to watch me cheer. He accompanied me on my dates. He kept special gold medals I'd earned from running track. As a lifeguard at the town pool, Bart sat by my chair enjoying my Coke. He trailed me and I loved it! He filled a void that all my achievements could not.

At eighteen, when I left for college, I felt as if I had abandoned my own son. Indeed, glancing behind me, I saw my eleven-year-old brother peddling his bike as fast as he could, yelling, "Please come home. I miss you!" It took everything I had not to turn around and take him with me.

Our mother remarried again and left the state, so I didn't see much of Bart during his high-school years. It wasn't until I got married, during his seventeenth summer, that our relationship had been rekindled. I lavishly praised him for receiving his GED, and for landing a job selling vacuums. Although he lived with

Mom seven hours away, he often spent the weekends with my husband and me at our condo.

One unexpected visit concerned me. His car broke down near my house, and he called to say he needed a place to stay. When I picked him up, something seemed different. He was distant and edgy. Later, when he learned his car would take two days to fix, he flew into a rage, then paced for hours.

Mom had told me she thought he was into drugs. Concerned, I sat Bart down and said, "I love you and I'm here for you. Mom has told me you are into cocaine, and I'm worried."

"Oh Suz," he replied as his nose crinkled, "You know Mom and her exaggerations. I'm fine. She can't tell me what to do anymore, and that makes her mad."

I couldn't deny that our mother loved to control her children, so I believed him. Still, when he drove off the next day, I had the fleeting thought, *I'll never see him again.*

I ignored the impulse to chase him as I raced to get to work on time. How could I have known this feeling was prophetic?

Days later, Bart was found dead in his car, along with drugs and a bizarre cassette tape in his tape recorder. With loud Mega-death heavy metal music in the background, Bart's slurred monologue began with a voice I didn't recognize, "Don't think that I didn't enjoy life, but death is the ultimate life has to offer!"

The tape abruptly stopped, and I can only surmise that he started the car and ended his life by carbon monoxide poisoning.

During those two silent days when Bart was missing, I prayed, "God, make him call! Please give me one more chance to talk to him."

The only call I received was from my stepfather who called on Bart's eighteenth birthday to inform me that Bart had committed suicide.

When I heard the news, I dropped the phone and started screaming like a wounded animal. Forty-five minutes later, when the neighbors knocked on the door to check on the noise, I stopped crying. Inwardly, however, I felt shame and guilt, and I missed my brother.

At the age of twenty-five, I clung to my belief in God like a drowning woman clutching a life preserver. My new husband and friends were encouraging but grew impatient, wondering, *What has happened to the "old Suzy"?*

"She's suffocating," I wanted to say but knew they wouldn't understand. By this time my support network expected healing, but the opposite occurred. I felt my raft of hope sinking!

Working hard at my sales job provided limited relief during the day. But sleepless nights became my enemy, and when I did doze, I experienced horrific nightmares. In these terrifying scenes I always arrived too late to rescue Bart and powerlessly watched him die. For the first time in my highly organized life, I was too tired to return phone calls, clean my house, or even wash my hair.

Meanwhile, I began to study the Bible through Bible Study Fellowship (BSF). I learned to apply Scripture to real-life situations. I read what Jesus said to Mary's accusers in Mark 14:8, "She did what she could" (NIV).

That spoke to me. It was like God said, "Sweet Suzy, you loved your brother. You did what you could. You couldn't have done anymore."

With this new peace of mind, I realized I had neglected my marriage. Suddenly my relationship with my husband flourished, and we decided to start our own family.

Becoming a mother myself, I pondered my own mom's accountability for this tragedy. Should I blame her multiple marriages for Bart's death? No, suicide happens in all types of families. Bart and I had shared the same family situations, and I hadn't killed myself.

I know I'll never understand Bart's life or why he felt the need to end it. But, in thinking about the vacuum cleaner struggling to clean my floor, I realized that just as time broke my vacuum, life broke Bart. His suicide almost destroyed me, but I now know that the responsibility for Bart's death rests on his own shoulders.

Tomorrow my three kids and I are going shopping. Ten years have passed, and I am finally ready to part with the sweeper that kept Bart's vivid memory alive. Bart will always hold a tender place in my heart, but the huge vacuum in my life caused by his death is being filled by the peace of Christ.

As I throw away the worn appliance, I'm ready to let go of the accountability for my brother and concentrate on God's gifts. I like to think that Bart is finally smiling.

What a Feast That Will Be!

Doris Schuchard

Leaving the doctor's office, I couldn't wait to share the news with my grandmother. Her first great-grandchild!

I could already imagine it! Grandmother would be waiting at the screen door, greeting each member of her family with a hug and a kiss. Fourteen family members gathered around the mahogany table, sampling turkey, German potato salad, and strawberry schaumtorte served on English bone china. After dinner we'd squeeze around the baby grand in the corner of the living room and join in singing Thanksgiving hymns. And in the midst of it all would be Grandmother, rocking the newest member of the family to sleep with German lullabies.

I never got to give Grandma my big announcement. A few weeks later, I listened to the pastor's words at her funeral, "Be faithful unto death, and I will give you the crown of life." Though her eighty years on earth were complete, Grandmother's new life had just begun.

I gazed at the wisps of white curls framing her face. "It wasn't time to leave, Grandma. There's a whole new generation coming who needs your wisdom," I whispered.

My aunt turned to comfort me with her embrace. "It seems whenever one of us is called home, a new life joins our family."

Even these hopes were not to be when I gave birth three months early. I stared for a moment into Daniel's cold blue eyes and stroked the tiny head that fit neatly into the palm of my hand. Hours later, he left as quickly as he came, his pain now replaced with peace.

My arms ached to hold my son, to introduce Daniel to his grandmothers and grandfathers, aunts and uncles. Instead, I stood at the gravesite for the second time, the familiar words echoing in my heart, "Be faithful unto death."

"But how is this possible, Lord?" I cried. "Daniel did not have the chance to live a long life. Is there a crown for his tiny head too?"

I realized then that it's not our length of life but God's grace that gives both an eighty-year-old saint and a one-day-old infant the same future of wholeness and joy.

It's not easy letting go of the people we love. Still, I've found that the gift is always greater to us. Grandma passed on a tradition of apple strudel and the heritage of a faithful walk. My son gave me both the joy and the pain of motherhood and the ability to reach out to others experiencing the same loss.

The biggest blessing is still to come. Yes, there may be empty chairs around the earthly table that will never be filled, but I look forward to an even greater family reunion, dining with my loved ones at that heavenly feast.

The Bleachers

Nancy I. Pamerleau

I remember vividly the moment, when twenty years ago, I met a stranger on the bleachers at a Little League game.

It was a breezy blue-sky day. Linda and I watched our skinny six-year-old daughters' timid first efforts at knocking a ball from a tee. The rural baseball diamond was surrounded by wild flowers, grass, and mature hardwoods. As we listened to the giggles of our children, Linda confided to me that she had a brain tumor. Somehow, in the beauty of the day, her death struggle didn't seem possible.

Over the next few summers, we regularly shared those bleachers, and Linda continued to tell me about her disease. There were times when I avoided her because I didn't want to hear it. At other times I listened as she described her seizures.

"I'm not supposed to drive, but I do anyway. I don't know what else to do. I have to get to work," she explained.

As a result of her seizures, Linda had several car crashes, and she often missed the games because of her illness. I was horrified when one sunny afternoon she shared, "My husband beats me because he's sick of hearing about my brain tumor."

I just didn't know how to respond.

Linda eventually divorced Nick and got custody of the girls; yet she worried about what would happen to her three daughters. She fought to live for their sakes but died before they all finished elementary school. I was dismayed to learn that their father got custody.

Every couple of years I see one of Linda's daughters and remember their mother's bravery, their father's cruelty, and my own lack of effort to make any difference.

Fifteen years after that season on the bleachers, my husband left me. Somehow, even through the pain, I felt a sense of relief. Though I had never been beaten like Linda, I understood cruel rejection. For instance, when I got glasses, my husband said, "Now the question is, will I still love you with glasses?"

Unfortunately, he did not.

Still, at forty-five-years-old, I relished being single. I had a career, a ministry on the college campus where I taught, and visions of becoming a missionary in some far-off place. "Alone" felt good. The fighting was finally over, and even the dog seemed to relax.

What did I need a man for? I managed beautifully by myself even though I did miss our old home near the lake where we raised our kids. Yet, God was present every day.

During that time, I begin to realize just how much God loved me. Though he wouldn't force my husband into wanting to repair our marriage, he had given me more than enough grace to face my days as a single person.

Then a dashing, freshly retired air force colonel came sweeping into my life. John immediately broke every stereotype of military rigidity. We laughed, fished, walked in the woods, picked berries, and ate cheap cheeseburgers.

The first gift he gave me was gift-wrapped box of bananas.

We went to church together, but I resisted the notion that a man could ever be a good thing in my life. I had always taken care of myself. Yet, it was nice to have someone helping me for a change.

I fought God hard and often. My life was fine. Who put this man in the way of my goals and plans? I sought the council of several ministers, other friends, and my dad. They all loved John too.

A sense of urgency developed about getting married quickly and living life fully. We were married three weeks after John proposed. We stood in front of the altar of a packed stone chapel by a lake surrounded with towering pines. The reception was held at the Officers' Club with a three-string orchestra. It was the storybook wedding I never had. In a few short years, we've laughed and played and served the church. We've searched out moose in Canada, snorkeled in Mexico, and walked the rim of a volcano. We've held hands as we've watched the deer play in our new yard.

God has restored what the canker worm had eaten. Even before John asked me to marry him, I knew that the worst day in my life with John would be better than any other day I had ever had. That was confirmed when what should have been the worst day of my life happened.

Like my friend Linda, now I'm the one with an inoperable, malignant brain tumor. And though I never had a servant's heart to help meet Linda's needs, God still forgave me and provided a servant's heart for me through John.

We will live each day we have left to the fullest, bonded by the love God has given to us for one another. How thankful I am to know such love.

12
Love Brings Joy

If I can stop one heart from breaking,
I shall not live in vain;
If I can ease one life the aching,
Or cool one pain,
Or help one fainting robin
Unto his nest again,
I shall not live in vain.

Emily Elizabeth Dickinson

The Christmas Tree Caper

Kimberly Lynn Frost

Christmas of 1986 was going to be tough. Money was scarce, and self-pity had moved into our home.

We looked for ways to cut our expenses for the season. Gifts, baking, decorating, trips—all were trimmed back. What else could we do? After discussing it, my husband Scott and I decided against getting a tree. We easily talked the kids—four-year-old Rebekah and two-year-old Jeremy—into the change of tradition. Together we decorated the houseplants instead. Our little home took on a modest but festive appearance.

A few days before Christmas, an acquaintance came to visit with her three-year-old son. He was quick to notice—and announce—how unlucky Rebekah and Jeremy were not to have a Christmas tree. My kids hadn't given "the tree thing" a second thought. But now they sulked for the next few days and looked at us with questioning eyes.

After we tucked the kids into bed on Christmas Eve, we finished some handmade things for them. By the time the ten o'clock news came on, we were finishing up when Scott blurted out, "The church!"

"What about the church?" I asked.

"The church has a Christmas tree!"

"So?"

"So, let's go get it."

"Are you crazy?"

"No, I'm not crazy. Get your keys!"

Scott and I were children's ministry leaders, so we had keys to the church. "We've been entrusted with keys for honorable things, not something like this," I warned.

Scott was not to be put off. He had the plan; I had the keys; and the church had the tree. Only a small snow-covered lot stood between our house and the church.

Dressed in sweats, boots, and coats and armed with a flashlight, we headed for the church. The more doubts plagued me, the more Scott's confidence kept building.

The key in the lock did not want to cooperate. As we fumbled about, my knees knocked from fear of discovery while Scott's shook from excitement. Finally, the key turned and we were in. The Christmas tree stood in a corner of the fellowship hall next to the piano.

"Stealing on Christmas Eve. In a church, no less! What will people think?" I whispered.

"We're not stealing, we're borrowing," Scott said.

"You still do time in jail for such borrowing, don't you?" I asked sheepishly.

We tipped the tree over carefully. Scott grabbed the trunk near the stand, and I held the top. We made our escape out the side door and headed for home.

A fully decorated Christmas tree does not travel well, even for such a short distance. The tree trimming began to unravel and fall in the snow. I was trying to pick up the shiny-colored Christmas balls that left a trail to our front door. Finally, Scott hoisted the tree up and carried it by himself.

Meanwhile, I continued to pull the Christmas balls out of the snow and stuff them in my bulging sweatshirt. As I walked in our door, I caught sight of the tree in the living room. Scott was ready to plug in the lights. The tree was beautiful and even more dazzling when we hung the ornaments that I retrieved from my sweatshirt. We both stood back and looked at it for a long, long time.

We were awakened Christmas morning with shouts of excitement. "Daddy! Mommy! We have a Christmas tree—with lights and silver things and big shiny Christmas balls." Scott and I jumped out of bed and joined in our kids' excitement.

Rebekah and Jeremy didn't seem to care about the gifts underneath the tree, even when we pointed them out. They had been given a tree! Suddenly, all the struggles of the past year and the strains of the coming year didn't really matter. We celebrated this Christmas Day with a different attitude.

That night, after Scott and I tucked the kids into bed and made sure they were asleep, we prepared to return the tree.

"What will we tell the kids when they ask where the tree went?" I asked, panicked.

"They won't. They'll understand," Scott said.

This time we took all the decorations off. I carried them in a big box while Scott took the tree. I found three ornaments still hidden in the snow on the return trip.

We set up and redecorated the tree in the fellowship hall where we had found it. Maybe it was my imagination, but, somehow, it seemed to stand just a little fuller than it had the night before.

The next morning, just as Scott had predicted, Rebekah and Jeremy never asked about the tree's whereabouts.

We later confessed to our pastor about our act of thievery. The following Christmas, amidst gales of laughter, he presented us with a reusable artificial tree. Still, every year we look at the church's Christmas tree and smile to ourselves. We remember the year the church's tree became our source of joy.

Lucky

Darlene Franklin

The bus stopped at a dark, deserted parking lot. Searching out the remaining Christmas lights in the distance, I misplaced a foot and slipped on the ice. My grocery bag tumbled to the ground. Just my luck! A high-pitched yelp cut through the air, distracting my attention. *What's that?*

"Meow." Clearer this time, a kitten in distress cried nearby. Retracing a few steps, I found a tiny ball of fur shivering by a parking lot bumper. Without hesitation, I scooped him up with one hand and placed the grocery bag in the other.

A lone dog began to bark as I walked by, and soon the entire neighborhood joined in on the litany. Tucked against my chest underneath my coat, the kitten shook with fright. "You're OK," I assured him. "You're safe for now. We'll find you a home—somehow." Five long blocks later, we made it to the apartment.

"Look what I found near the bus stop," I said to my daughter Jolene who was waiting for me at the house. By the light we took a good look: a male kitten, maybe six weeks old, elegant in black and white. Soon he was racing around the kitchen as if he owned it.

"Let's call him Lucky," Jolene suggested. "Like the puppy—"

"In *101 Dalmatians.* Perfect." I agreed.

"Lucky Spot," she decided. "Because of the white spot on his chest."

We introduced Lucky Spot to our cats. Andres, a thirty-pound male, sniffed at him curiously. The older female, Puff, howled with menace and stood guard over the food dish. She confirmed what I already suspected: we couldn't keep another cat in our small apartment.

"We'll put up 'Found' signs. If no one claims him in a week, we'll have to take him to a shelter." I cuddled Lucky Spot in my hands and stroked his fur. A loud purr rocked his body. "How could anyone abandon him? He's a sweetie."

The phone rang. It was Maria, a friend from church, someone who seldom called. "Sorry I missed you on Sunday." We chatted for a couple of minutes. Lucky climbed to my shoulder, knocking away the receiver. I disentangled his determined claws and set him back on the floor.

"Sorry about that." I apologized. "I had a kitten trying to crawl down my back."

"I remember when Henry used to do that." Maria referred to her own tortoise-shell cat.

"How's he doing these days?"

"He died over Christmas." Sadness colored her words.

By my foot Lucky Spot played with my shoestring. *Of course!*

"Then would you like a kitten? We found a stray tonight and . . ."

Before I could finish the sentence, she interrupted, "When can we pick him up?"

We all received what we needed that night. A lost cat found a new home. A grieving friend adopted a new pet to love. And me? I was lucky enough to bring them together.

Heart of the Giver

Roberta Updegraff

Every year I make a resolution not to get caught up in the fervor of creating the perfect family Christmas and end up disappointed when reality doesn't match the fantasies I fabricate from the covers of women's magazines. This season I asked God to help me stay focused on him.

Christmas day my family gathered at the home of my mother-in-law for the traditional family brunch. Although there had been promises not to buy gifts for one another, no one had been able to resist "a little something" for each person there. To my disgrace, I was the only one who'd kept the promise! Pride snarled inside of me, tying my stomach in knots, and the sour taste of it stung the back of my throat.

As I wrestled that monster, the teenagers chattered expectations of the latest fads and designer labels, while the younger children soared on a tinsel and wrapping paper high. And I became more and more convinced that this would be another Christmas gone wrong; once again, I'd miss out on the joy that was supposed to accompany this season. But then I remembered; the morning had been so hectic that I had forgotten to pray. I had lost focus.

I closed my eyes and quieted my mind. As I welcomed Peace into my soul, the room became warmer and the scent of pine more distinct. I asked God to renew a right spirit within me and found myself able to accept, guilt-free, the gifts from extended family. I even let myself enjoy the pleasure they took in giving what they said was "a perfect little something"—a token of their love and respect for me.

Then my mother-in-law brought into the room four large wrapped boxes—one for each family. Sensing something important was about to happen, the children gathered at the feet of their parents as Gram explained how she'd waited for years to present these gifts. As each of her children was given the honor of opening a package, an anticipatory hush enveloped us, and I leaned back in my chair, recognizing that this was a memory in the making. Was this the experience for which my prayers had been offered?

"What do you think it is?" whispered my youngest, eyes dancing with wonder.

Although I shrugged, I, too, was almost giddy with excitement.

The air prickled with the rustle of paper until all the recipients held the boxes on their laps, each waiting for the others. As we sat for that moment of delight, rapted in hallowed silence, I scanned the room trying to memorize each facial expression, knowing I'd remember it forever.

My mother-in-law's weathered features softened with a youthful glow, and a smile lit her eyes. Leaning forward on the chair, she could hardly keep her hands still, seeming to mentally unwrap the treasures. As the lids were lifted, she fussed over whether she'd chosen the right colors for each family. I saw her blush as we showered her with praise, and though she tried hard to hide it, our usually stoic matriarch was practically bursting with joy.

It had taken her ten years to construct these cherished quilts. Each one consisted of twelve panels of an intricate arrangement called Mariner's Compass; every one a harmony of pattern and color. Delicate quilting stitches, an art within an art, were framed by perfect corners attesting to a master's craftsmanship.

She was giving away more than a hand-crafted original. She had spent countless hours in this labor of love, and with each meticulously executed stitch, she'd pieced together fabric and spirit. I pictured her sitting in her favorite chair with the quilting frame on her lap, anticipating this very day, having planned the color schemes with each family in mind. Though she'd never been good at saying the words "I love you," when my gaze met hers, I could see her heart.

That evening our five-year-old daughter ran to Daddy with her almost-forgotten present. She, too, had created a masterpiece: a small clay pot. Strangely, I'd never seen the family resemblance between our youngest daughter and her grandmother. But as I watched her stand at Daddy's knee, hurrying him with chubby fingers ripping at the homemade wrapping paper, it was all too familiar—the delight in her eye, anticipation in her body language, and sweet babbling to hide vulnerability at the fear that her gift might not be as special as she'd thought.

I closed my eyes again, this time to thank God for redirecting my focus as he recalled in me something forgotten. Though I, too, knew the thrill and the satisfaction of seeing my gifts delight loved ones, I'd been so busy making sure this season went "just right" that

I had lost my joy. I smiled, warmed to my very being. This had become the perfect family Christmas.

I watched our little one being hugged by her father; the smile lighting her eyes confirmed it. Love at its best was vulnerable.

I cannot match my gift-givers' extravagant generosity, but I will graciously accept their gifts of love, thus allowing myself to be stitched by grace into an heirloom quilt—a harmony of pattern and color.

With all my love, I will pass that quilt on to my children.

The Easter Gift

D. J. Cramer

The sun was shining on the warm spring day. Trees were budding with the first hint of the summer to come. Delicate yellow flowers hung on the forsythia beside the front door, while daffodils peeked through the last remnants of snow from the blizzard the week before. The Easter bunny had come and gone, and the children laughed as they bounced around the living room waiting impatiently for company to arrive.

The gaunt man shuffled slowly up the stairs to the front door, a white plastic sack in his hand. I greeted my younger brother warmly, glad to see him, but subdued by the sadness that gripped my heart whenever I saw him. The musty odor that always clung to his clothes followed him into the house. He had done his best to clean up for the occasion, but the stubble of a graying beard still cast a shadow on his face, and his thinning hair straggled around his haunted eyes.

"A present for the children," he said in the mumbling, slightly embarrassed way he had of speaking about anything that touched his heart. The children hung back a little, eager to see what the surprise package held, yet hesitant to embrace their disheveled uncle. He often brought them presents and made them laugh. Still, they always knew that something was not quite right. Their reluctance vanished quickly, replaced by big smiles and cheerful greetings, for they knew he was welcome here.

The bag was set aside behind the living room chair to be opened later in the day. Now we needed to leave for the Easter services at the church, a family tradition. For the first time in years, my brother was going with us. Unspoken thoughts hung in the air. Do we dare go to church together? Is he well enough to deal with the profound emotion awaiting him there? Will people make him feel welcome? Will he think they are staring at him? Will he get too anxious in the crowd?

All of these questions weighed heavily on my heart, but I knew that this time he wanted to be there. And we had come to an understanding through years of struggle. He would be responsible for telling me if the situation was becoming too difficult for him to tolerate. I would respect his discomfort by leaving immediately to take him home, no matter where we were or what we were doing. Only in this way had he managed to share in our lives for so many years.

"Hallelujahs" echoed through the air, announcing to the world that love triumphs and hope lives. Sunlight streaming through stained-glass windows filled the little alcove with rainbow colors. The subtle perfume of white lilies lingered in the air. A simple cross hung in the background, entwined with palm leaves and white carnations.

My brother sat stiffly in the small side pew, hidden from full view of the cheerful faces that filled the small church. His gaze was fixed on the words of the hymn book in his hands, trembling visibly as they turned the pages. I didn't dare look directly in his eyes for fear that we would both start to cry. Instead,

I gently laid my hand in his to reassure him that he could make it through this day.

"He is risen. He is risen," the pastor declared. "He is risen indeed," responded the congregation. "And he promises eternal life to all who gather here. Come kneel at the cross. Let your hearts be still. Leave your sins and sorrow at Christ's feet. Ask for forgiveness and forgive. Receive the gift of bread and wine. Feel God's blessing touch your head."

I did not know if my brother would join me for Communion, but he rose unsteadily when the usher came to our pew and stood straight and tall in the line. This time I could not stop the tears that rushed down my cheeks. For I knew that he had not been able to come this far for a long time.

We knelt together, side by side, each with sorrow deep in our hearts—the Vietnam veteran, his life racked with pain, his mind slipping daily beyond his own control—and the sister he had always relied on to help him, unable to stop the illness that ravaged his spirit. The world could not help him; only God offered hope and comfort now. Seeing his hand tremble, I touched it once more. I knew what great courage it took for him to be there and understood how much it mattered to him this Easter morning.

Quiet settled between us when we returned to our seats. As Communion continued, I said a silent prayer: *Father in heaven, we have no hope but that which is promised us this Easter day. We ask for forgiveness for lives we may have hurt, for love unexpressed. We have no power to change what has occurred or make this ill-*

*ness disappear from this world. We long for the peace
the Lord grants to those who kneel at his feet. Amen.*

The noon sun was warm as we left the church. "If
I get lost, do you think the Lord will come find me, like
the pastor said?" my brother asked. "Yes," I replied.
That was all he said about the service; it seemed to be
enough.

As we entered the house, the children headed
straight for the mysterious bag. "Let's go to the park,"
their uncle said. His gift was meant to be used outdoors, where there was plenty of room to run. "Let's
go," the children agreed.

The park was filled with babies and children, parents and puppies, and ducks on the lake. Puffy clouds,
pushed along by a gentle breeze, drifted through the
sky. "Open the package," the children cried. "Let's see
what you brought us. It's time for your surprise."

He slowly opened the sack and pulled out a kite
like none they had ever seen. It was a Chinese kite of
brilliant colors—red, purple, yellow, blue, and green.
He had found it on one of his many trips to
Woolworth's. Made of stiff cellophane, the kite crackled and popped as he proudly pulled it out of its makeshift wrapping. It looked like a dragon, with its large
circular body and long streamer tail.

"Run, Uncle Paul. Lift it up in the air. Let's see if it
flies," the children squealed with delight. Then he ran
and he laughed until he fell to the ground, rolling over
and over like the child he had been long ago. He
smiled as he ran; his eyes glowed as he laughed. This
moment was precious; he was peaceful at last.

On this wonderful day, the joy Paul longed for was his. It would vanish soon enough in the long, lonely hours to follow, as the voices that haunted his mind shrieked through the night. But for now he could run; he could laugh; he could play. He had shared God's gift of love this Easter day.

Enjoy the View

Phillip Van Hooser

A recent father-daughter trout fishing excursion found me at the base of a north Georgia mountain with my eight-year-old daughter, Sarah. Brasstown Bald Mountain, reportedly the highest point in the state of Georgia at 4,784 feet, loomed over us.

After driving to the mountain's visitor reception area, we were informed that if we wanted to experience the true magnificence of the mountain, we had to hike a near vertical, half-mile trail to the summit.

"Do you want to try?" I asked Sarah.

Sarah pondered the question, then nodded. Then, with a quick exchange of smiles, we were off on our merry journey.

Soon, our perfect father-daughter adventure became an exhausting effort. The climb was tough and unrelenting. Sarah and I tired quickly, stopping several times to catch our breath before we struggled on.

Finally, after more than thirty long, hard minutes of hiking, we emerged from the mountain's forest. Tired, but thrilled to be so close to achieving our goal, we staggered onward to the summit. The result was a breathtaking view. A 360-degree panoramic view of the countryside lay peacefully before us. Under a beautiful blue sky, we stood silently, soaking up the extraordinary sight.

"It's beautiful," Sarah exclaimed, still panting slightly.

I reached for her hand and squeezed it. "It sure is!"

We sat together on a flat gray stone overlooking the view, feeling the warmth of the sun on our faces. I asked, "Sarah, what does this climb teach us?"

Sarah thought for a moment. Finally, she tilted her head and asked, "It's beautiful at the top?"

"That's true, but there's more. It's not just beautiful at the top; it's beautiful all the way to the top."

I gestured at the grandeur below. "We passed all these things on our way up. We either drove or hiked past the same mountains and valleys, lakes and streams, towns and farms that we see now."

"You're right," Sarah mused as she let the breeze play through her hair.

I added, "It seems we were so busy trying to get to the top that we missed the beauty of the journey."

After enjoying the splendor of our overlook, the two of us began our leisurely hike back down to the base. On the return trip, Sarah and I heard the call of the mockingbird. We noticed the beauty of the moss-covered rocks, the towering trees, and the tiny, shy violets. Majesty was everywhere.

I remember hearing Chuck Swindoll once say, "Wherever you are—be all there!" I am trying to apply that simple philosophy in my life and work. I am learning to truly give myself over as I tune into a conversation with my children, a friend, or an audience member. I find the beauty around me comes into clearer, deeper focus. The result is that my personal journey toward my "mountaintops" is peppered with experiences of beauty and love. Somehow that makes my strenuous climb an adventure to appreciate. The majesty is everywhere.

A Rainbow's Promise

LeAnn Thieman

"MaiLy! Wake up, little one!" the nun said in a frantic whisper. MaiLy rubbed her sleepy eyes with the back of her hand. "Wake! Hurry!" Sister Katrine grasped her arm and pulled her to a sitting position. "It's time!"

Time for what? Mai wondered as she obediently stood beside her cot and watched Sister wake the other nine-year-olds in the same way. She nudged them toward Mai, then to the door and into the black night. Explosions sounded in the distance.

Whimpering children from other cottages rushed past them down the dirt path. Mai ran with them to the main gate of the orphanage where they shivered in silence. They heard the familiar rumble of Vietnamese army vehicles, then gunfire blasts nearby. Huddling closer, they wrapped their arms around each other as tanks thundered past the gate. The vibration shook through their bones. Repeated gunfire blazed sudden bursts of light against a pitch black curtain of night as the explosions grew nearer. The trembling children cried softly. Sister Katrine opened the gate a few inches.

"The war is here, my children. Do not be afraid. God will save us, but we must run for safety now." One by one, she coaxed the frightened children out the gate and commanded them to run to the convent at the top of the hill.

"Run!" she yelled as she shoved Mai through the gate.

"Run! Run! Run!" Mai commanded herself as her

bare feet pounded the earth. Bombs exploded like fireworks, providing the only light as she stumbled along the rocky path. The sky became brighter as the bombing increased, but smoke clouded her way. She tried to suppress the sobs that spent her diminishing breath.

"Run! Run! Run!" she repeated to herself. Her tears tasted like dirt as she wiped them with her grimy hand. When she reached the convent, she ascended the stairs two at a time, then crouched in the corner and waited for the other children.

Soon an army truck pulled up. "Come! Hurry!" the nun commanded. A Vietnamese soldier pulled back the canvas canopy and boosted the children into the back of the truck two and three at a time. When the bench seats were full, the remaining children crowded together on the floor. The truck lunged forward, and their treacherous journey to freedom began. Mai cuddled closer to her friends and wondered if she would see the orphanage, or the American who had promised to come back for her, ever again.

The truck snaked its way through the chaos of war and eventually to a coastal city. There the nuns and children sought refuge in a church. Hesitantly, Sister Katrine approached Mother Superior and told her of her plan to leave with MaiLy.

"Absolutely not!" the older nun hissed.

But Sister Katrine insisted. "I must try to get her to Saigon, then to the American GI who has waited for seven years to adopt her." Looking into her superior's eyes, she repeated firmly. "With or without your consent, I am taking MaiLy."

With the sun setting to her back, Sister Katrine

gripped Mai's hand and raced eastward toward the shore. Her habit hiked to her knees, Sister Katrine assisted in building a tiny raft on which she, Mai, and a dozen frantic people crowded. As their rig pushed off at sunset and drifted into the South China Sea, they looked back at a city on fire.

Sister placed MaiLy in a cardboard box, but it was flimsy protection against the tempestuous sea. Wind and mountainous waves lashed at the raft, threatening to consume it and the refugees on board. The deafening roar drowned out hollered commands and prayers.

For hours the ruthless waves battered their bodies relentlessly, and they fought to keep from being devoured by the monstrous sea. The sun's slow descent on the horizon seemed to steal the power from the storm. Then a vibrant rainbow appeared. "That's a sign of God's promise," Sister whispered to MaiLy. "He will protect you from life's storms."

Days later, the raft docked in Saigon. Sister Katrine and MaiLy joined the throngs of panicking people in overloaded carts, oxen, and scooters racing for their freedom. Miraculously, Sister Katrine found the agency that had wanted to facilitate Mai's adoption. There, Sister squatted to Mai's level. "Do you remember the special American GI who came to visit you many times at the orphanage?" Mai nodded. "He lives far away. If I leave you here, they will take you to him."

"But I don't want you to leave me," Mai whimpered, stepping closer to her.

Sister took a handkerchief from her sleeve and wiped her eyes. "Haven't I always taken good care of you, MaiLy?"

Mai nodded again.

"Now I can take the best care of you by letting you go."

Mai wrapped her arms around Sister Katrine's neck.

Sister whispered, "Remember, God will take care of you; he will give you rainbows after the storms." Then she took Mai's hand and led her to the steps of the orphan evacuation center. Mai waved goodbye to the only family she had ever known.

The next day, Mai was loaded on board a gutted cargo jet with one hundred other children. Babies were placed two and three to a cardboard box with toddlers and older children sitting on the side bench seats. As the plane lifted off the ground, Mai pressed her face against the window. Her tears trickled down the glass.

Babies gently bumped against each other when the plane landed in the Philippines. All the children were escorted to Clark Air Force Base in open-air buses. Mai leaned her head against the window and gazed solemnly at the scenery. The palm trees seemed to wave a tranquillity unknown in Vietnam.

There was no congestion of carts, scooters, or oxen.

No thunderous bombings,
No hordes of frightened people,
But no orphanage,
No Sister Katrine, and—
No American GI.

Mai spent most of the next two days curled up on her mattress at Operation Babylift headquarters.

Hundreds of children ran merrily and joined in games as they waited for a larger, safer plane to complete their journey. Mai lay curled, ignoring the kind acts of her volunteer caregivers. Feeling betrayed and abandoned, she wondered if she would ever see her friends, her homeland, or the American GI again. She recalled the day, when she was three, that she saw him the first time. It was then she had chosen him. Clinging to his leg, she sat on his foot for a "ride" as he diapered and fed the babies. She closed her eyes and remembered swinging on his lap on the old rope swing in the dusty playground. She could almost feel his whiskers on her face as she did when she pressed her cheek to his in their usual hug. A smile crossed her lips as she relived the day he brought dozens of balloons and kazoos to the orphanage. He had handed a kazoo to each child and motioned for the children to watch him as he hummed into his. They all followed suit, spraying spit and slobber without song. Laughing, he showed them again and again until the room vibrated with the sounds of joyful children blasting their tunes. Mai rolled over on her mattress and sighed, wondering why he hadn't come back for her as he had promised.

Over and over again Mai asked that question. The answer, "America," was meaningless to her.

The next day she and the three hundred children were loaded onto a mammoth plane with dozens of volunteers. Again she asked the question. Again they answered, "America."

After several more plane flights and bus rides, the answer was, "Denver." Mai stepped off the bus with the other children and ascended a flight of stairs to yet another gathering place for the war orphans. She sulked into the room and heard a man call out breathlessly, "MaiLy!"

And there he was.

The American GI she had chosen in Vietnam ran to her, swooping her into his arms. He twirled her as she pressed her cheek to his in their familiar hug. He took her home that same evening where she was welcomed by his wife, his two little girls, sugared Cheerios, and Mickey Mouse sheets.

As she cuddled with her daddy on an over-stuffed sofa, multicolored snowflakes glistened in the moonlight on the window pane. Sister Katrine was right—there are rainbows at the end of the storms.

About Linda Evans Shepherd

Linda, the 1997 Colorado Christian author of the year, is the author of nine books, including *Heart-Stirring Stories of Romance* (Broadman & Holman) and *Encouraging Hands, Encouraging Hearts* (Servant). She coauthored *Share Jesus without Fear* with Bill Fay (Broadman & Holman) and is a member of the National Speakers Association and CLASS. She has been married for more than twenty years and has two children.

Linda makes her audiences laugh and cry as she shares her own stories. She reminds us that *Faith Never Shrinks in Hot Water* and *God Wants Spiritual Fruit Not Religious Nuts* and teaches us *How to Make Time* for our friends, family, and a relationship with God. She may be available for your next retreat or special event.

To check Linda's availability and fees, go online to: http://www.sheppro.com or call Speak Up Speaker Services at (888) 870-7719 or CLASSServices at (800) 433-6633.

Do you have a story of romance, faith, love, or hope to tell for a future book? If so, please send it to Linda at:

Heart-Stirring Stories
Attn: Linda Evans Shepherd
P.O. Box 6421
Longmont, CO 80501

or E-mail (paste into the text of your E-mail to Linda at): Lswrites@aol.com.

For editorial guidelines, check Linda's web page at http://www.sheppro.com, or send a self-addressed, stamped envelope to the address listed above.

Permissions

"Anguish in the Night," © by Jerry B. Jenkins, was originally published in *Moody* magazine; used by permission.

"The Rose Bush" was adapted from *When the Honeymoon's Over* by Kathy Collard Miller and D. Larry Miller, pages 45–46, © 1997 and used by permission of Harold Shaw Publishers, Wheaton, IL 60189.

"Are You God" was taken from *Improving Your Serve* by Charles R. Swindoll, © 1981, Word Publishing, Nashville, Tennessee; all rights reserved.

"Love Listens" was taken from *Heartbeat,* © 1991 Jill Briscoe, Harold Shaw Publishers; used with permission.

"What's Your Name?" was taken from *As Refreshing as Snow in the Hot Summertime,* © 1998 by Joanne Wallace and Deanna Wallace, published by Joanne Wallace, 1825 S.W. Coast Ave., Lincoln City, Oregon 97367-2124; used by permission.

"I Want That One" was taken from *How to Keep the Kids on Your Team* by Charles Stanley, © 1997, Thomas Nelson Publishers; used with permission.

"Death's Colors" was reprinted from *Whispers from Heaven* by Dayle Allen Shockley, © 1994 by Pacific Press Publishing Association.

"How Big Is God?," "Letters to Death Row," and "Getting Carried Away," were reprinted from *Faith Never Shrinks in Hot Water,* © 1996 Linda E. Shepherd, Pacific Press Publishing Association.

Contributors

I wish to thank the following people who graciously shared their lives with us:

Charlotte Adelsperger is a speaker and the author of three books as well as numerous articles and poems. Her credits include *Decision, Pray,* and *A Second Chicken Soup for the Woman's Soul.* She gives thanks for her sister, Alberta Heil, whose experiences are shared in this book. You may contact Charlotte at 11629 Riley, Overland Park, KS 66210. Phone: 913-345-1678.

Andria Anderson lives in Chicago with her husband, three children, and three foster teens. When not teaching piano or restoring their large Victorian home, she hides at the computer. There she records the mishaps of the household and edits them so they're believable. Contact her at AAnder87@aol.com.

Marlene Bagnull is a wife, mother of three adult children, and author of seven books, including *My Turn to Care—Encouragement for Caregivers of Aging Parents* and *Write His Answer—A Bible Study for Christian Writers.* She directs the Greater Philadelphia and Colorado Christian Writers conferences. You may contact her at mbagnull@aol.com.

Nancy Bayless is a seasoned award-winning writer with numerous articles in Christian magazines and newspapers, as well as two *Guidepost* books. She is an active member of the San Diego County Christian Writers Guild, a great-grandmother, and a world sailor.

Elena Bowman, novelist and short story writer, has completed six full-length novels, three nonfiction books, and thirty-three short stories. Past president and treasurer of the Massachusetts chapter of the National League of

American PenWomen, she is the current president of the Merrimack Valley Chapter of that organization. You may contact her at elenab@ne.mediaone.net and/or access http://people.ne.mediaone.net/elenab/index.html.

Jill Briscoe is a popular speaker and has authored more than forty books. She serves as advisor to the Women's Ministries at Elmbrook Church in Brookfield, Wisconsin, where her husband, Stuart, serves as pastor. She is executive director of *Just Between Us,* a magazine for ministry wives and women in ministry. Her TV program, "Bridges," can be seen on cable TV. She and Stuart minister together through Telling the Truth media ministries.

Georgia Burkett is a grandmother and great-grandmother. She clowns occasionally for children's programs and sings with a group of "over 55'ers" who refuse to grow old, for nursing homes, senior centers, and various churches. Her E-mail address is georgiab2@juno.com.

Janice Byrd is a public speaker, oral book reviewer, librarian, and freelance writer, who lives in McKinney, Texas. She may be reached at JaniceByrd@ConsultingPros.com.

Jack Cavanaugh is the author of the award-winning American Family Portrait series, of which *The Puritans* won a Silver Medallion. His most recent novel, *Glimpses of Truth,* is gaining national media attention. A popular inspirational speaker, Jack and his wife Marni live in southern California. He can be contacted at wjackc@home.com.

Jan Coleman likes to encourage her audiences that God "will restore to you the years that the locust hath eaten" (Joel 2:25). When she's not writing, she and husband Carl are budget travelers off to see and appreciate God's world. She'd love to hear from you: jwriter@foothill.net.

Ken Davis is a sought-after speaker, appearing on television and stage around the world. He's the host of a popular daily radio show, "Lighten Up," heard on more than five hundred stations across the country. He has written seven books, including *How to Live with Your Parents without Losing Your Mind* and *How to Live with Your Kids When You've Already Lost Your Mind.* His numerous awards include the Campus Life "Book of the Year" and the CBA Gold Medallion.

Mimi Deeths is a wife and mother of four young adult children. Residing in Bakersfield, California, she especially enjoys family gatherings when the kids return from various university campuses for a home-cooked meal. She brings a unique perspective to patients and their families who are facing cancer.

Betsy Dill, an illustrator of children's books and cartoons, turned to writing later in life. Her inspirational articles and humor columns have appeared in magazines and newspapers. A former homeschooling mother, she now freelances out of her home studio in Centerville, Virginia.

Darlene Franklin's work has appeared in *Parenttalk, Secret Place,* and the *American Reference Books Annual.* Heartsong Presents is considering her contemporary inspirational romances, *Romanian Rhapsody* and *PlainSong.* Ms. Franklin is a founding member of All Write Away and Colorado Writers Fellowship. She can be reached at 303-783-8915.

Kimberly Frost lives, works, and writes atop Grand Mesa in Colorado. She has authored more than one hundred short stories appearing in *The Christian Reader, The Fence Post,* and local area publications. You may contact her at sfrost3@co.tds.net.

Natalie Nicole Gilbert has authored articles, stories, and poems for a variety of publications, including the book *Pinches of Salt, Prisms of Light,* and *Southeast Outlook Newspaper.* Natalie speaks daily on the air at WQFL in Rockford, Illinois, as morning show cohost, in addition to leading retreats and conferences. Natalie can be reached at NatalieNicole@jewishmail.com.

Roy Hanschke is a writer, speaker, trainer, and Christian radio personality in Denver, where he is heard on KWBI FM 91.1. Roy also owns Voice Personality, a company that develops products and services for improving the speaking voice. His writing includes inspirational stories, curriculum, and articles for speaking voice improvement. He teaches radio and television announcing at the university level. Roy lives in Littleton, Colorado, where he and his wife Ruth enjoy their children, grandchildren, and the beautiful Rocky Mountains. Contact info: ruroi@aol.com, 1-800-604-8843.

Bonnie Compton Hanson, writer, editor, artist, and poet, has authored several books, including a Gold Medallion finalist for children. Her lively family includes husband Don, children, grandchildren, and assorted pets. You may reach Bonnie at 3330 S. Lowell St., Santa Ana, CA 92707; phone: 714-751-7824; E-mail: bonnieh1@worldnet.att.net.

Nancy Hoag is a wife, mother, and grandmother with more than eight hundred published articles and devotions to her credit. In addition, she is the author of three books, including *Good Morning! Isn't It a Fabulous Day?,* and *Storms Pass, So Hang On!* (both with Beacon Hill Press of Kansas City). Nancy is also a frequent speaker and teacher at writers' conferences and women's retreats.

Jo Huddleston is the author of three books, *Amen and Good Morning, God; Amen and Good Night, God;* and *His Awesome Majesty,* and numerous articles that have appeared in such national magazines as *Guideposts* and *Decision.* Jo is a book reviewer and conference workshop speaker. Contact her at johudd@earthlink.net.

Stan Jantz is the public relations manager for Berean Christian Stores. He has coauthored more than a dozen books with Bruce Bickel, including *Bruce & Stan's Guide to God* and *God Is in the Small Stuff.* Two of Bruce and Stan's books are Gold Medallion Award finalists. You may contact Stan at guide@bruceandstan.com.

Jennifer Jones, mother of two college students, works as a communication technician and a freelance writer. She's a member of SCBWI, and her stories and devotional meditations have appeared in several children's and teen magazines.

Nancy Kennedy lives in Inverness, Florida, with her husband Barry and youngest daughter Laura. She loves her job as the religion reporter of her local newspaper and editor of a monthly magazine for senior citizens. Her latest book is *Prayers God Always Answers* (WaterBrook Press).

Virelle Kidder is a full-time writer and conference speaker. She's also a contributing editor for *Today's Christian Woman* and the author of three books, including *Loving, Launching, and Letting Go* and *Getting the Best Out of Public Schools,* coauthored with her husband Steve, an educational psychologist. You may contact her at VBKidder@juno.com.

Kathy Collard Miller is a popular speaker and best-selling author of forty books, including *Through His Eyes.* She can be reached at http:/www.larryandkathy.com.

Carmen Leal-Pock is an author, singer, and CLASS graduate. She speaks in churches, conventions, and conferences throughout the country. She is the author of *Faces of Huntington's,* a book for and about people with Huntington's disease and others who care, and she coauthored *Pinches of Salt, Prisms of Light.* You may contact her at Carmen@Leal.com.

Eddie Ogan and her husband live in the mountains, on a creek, in a log cabin they built themselves. They have one child by birth, seventy-seven foster children, and eleven adopted children. They have sixteen grandchildren and nine great-grandchildren. She enjoys writing monthly to more than one hundred missionary families.

Nancy Pamerleau speaks at retreats and conferences. She is the author of numerous articles and a book on public speaking. She teaches at Kirtland Community College in Roscommon, Michigan. You may contact her at pamerlen@k2.kirtland.cc.mi.us.

Dr. Terry Paulson of Agoura Hills, California, is the 1998-99 president of the National Speakers Association and coauthored with son, Sean, *Can I Have the Keys to the Car?: How Teens and Parents Can Talk about Things That Really Matter* (Augsburg Fortress 1999). Terry helps leaders and teams make change work. Contact him at 818-991-5110 or DrTerryP@aol.com. Visit http://www.changecentral.com.

Carol McAdoo Rehme, an energetic storyteller and freelance writer, is a guest speaker at conferences, workshops, libraries, schools, and museums. Her professional affiliations include the National Storytelling Association, Northern Colorado Storytellers, Society of Children's Book Writers and Illustrators, and Writer's Critique. Contact her at

2503 Logan Dr., Loveland, CO, 80538, 970-669-5791, or E-mail her at rehme@verinet.com.

Naomi Rhode, a speaker, author, and corporate executive, has impacted and challenged audiences on the worldwide platform. She reveals compelling reasons and results for leadership, empowerment, teamwork, service, communication, and successful interpersonal relationships. Her emphasis is "Moving People from Success to Significance." She is a past president of the National Speakers Association, CSP, CPAE Speaker's Hall of Fame, as well as a Cavett Award winner.

Suzy Ryan lives in southern California with her husband and three small children. Her articles have appeared in *Decision, TCW, Woman's World, the American Enterprise, Bounce Back Too,* and various newspapers. You can reach her at KenSuzyR@aol.com.

Carolyn R. Scheidies writes print novels for Barbour Publishing and electronic novels for Mountain View Publishing. She also has an audiobook released by PIA. Carolyn is past president of the local public library "Friends of the Library" organization and works with a puppet team in Kearny, Nebraska. She also presents workshops and speaks to different groups. Contact her at www.pages.ivillage/bc/crscheidies.

Renee Coates Scheidt is a gifted communicator. Whether speaking, singing, or writing, she knows how to connect with her audience. She is a member of the National Speakers Association, CLASS, and the Coalition of Southern Baptist Music Evangelists. She resides in her home state of North Carolina.

Doris Schuchard is a wife and mother of two children. She is a freelance writer in the areas of family and education. She recently moved from the Midwest to Atlanta, where she enjoys the year-round flowers as well as the friendliness of everyone she meets.

Dayle Shockley, an inspirational writer and speaker, is the author of *Whispers from Heaven* and *Silver Linings* (Pacific Press). Her work has appeared in more than thirty periodicals, including *Guideposts, Focus on the Family, Moody, Houston Chronicle, the Dallas Morning News,* and *Catholic Digest.*

Doris Smalling, published poet, author, and public speaker, teaches an adult Sunday school class. She is a wife, mother of three grown children, and a volunteer tutor. She won the Valley Forge Freedoms Foundation Poetry/Drama Award. Contact her at dpsmalling@aol.com or write her at 1137 N. Harrison Ct., E. Wenatchee, WA 98802.

Lauraine Snelling is the award winning author of thirty-five novels, including the Red River of the North series, *Dakota, Hawaiian Sunrise,* and two series for young girls who love horses, the Golden Filly series and *High Hurdles.* Lauraine teaches at writers seminars across the country and is a popular speaker as well. Contact for Lauraine is TLSnelling@AOL.com.

Marti Suddarth is a freelance writer and composer of children's musicals, including *A Visit with Jane Q. Offeringbox.* She is a member of the writers' group, SALT. Marti and her husband Daniel have been married since 1985 and have three children, Katie, Scott, and Abby. You may contact her at asksuddarth@juno.com.

LeAnn Thieman helped rescue three hundred babies during the Vietnam Orphan Airlift. Now a nationally acclaimed speaker and author, she inspires audiences to balance their lives and truly live their priorities while making a difference in the world. To inquire about her book, tapes, and live presentations, contact her at www.LeAnnThieman.com or 1-877-THIEMAN.

Nanette Thorsen-Snipes has at least 250 articles, columns, stories, and devotions in more than thirty-five publications, including: *Honor Books, Christian Reader, Positive Living* magazine, *Breakaway, Home Life, Publications International, Inc., Georgia* magazine, *Accent on Living, Southern Lifestyles, Experiencing God, Power for Living,* and others. Contact: P.O. Box 1596, Buford, GA, 30515; or jsnipes212@aol.com.

Roberta Updegraff's most important profession is that of homemaker. She has been happily married for twenty-five years and enjoys her two teenaged daughters and college-aged son. She is a substitute teacher, youth leader, and freelance writer. She has sold to numerous magazines, including *Focus on the Family, Moody, Group Publishing, Virtue, Christian Educator, Christian Communicator,* and *Overdrive* (popular magazine in the trucking industry). She is currently working on a missionary biography for Christian Publications, serves on the board of St. David's Christian Writer's Conference and is involved with the West Branch Christian Writers organization.

Phillip Van Hooser, CSP, delivers business keynotes and training development programs addressing leadership, change, team building, and service professionalism. The author of *You're Joe's Boy, Ain't Ya?, Life's Lessons for Living, Loving, and Leading,* Phil is a member of the National Speakers Association. Contact Phil at phil@vanhooser.com.

Barbara Vogelgesang speaks and performs throughout the world. She has toured with Ringling Brothers

Barnum & Bailey Circus, is a CLASS graduate, and holds a journalism degree from St. John's University, NYC. She and her husband are the proud parents of two children. You may contact her at joyousheart@juno.com.

Joanne Wallace speaks at Christian conferences/retreats and seminars. She's the author of nine books, including *As Refreshing as Snow in the Hot Summertime.* She is a member of the National Speakers Association and holds the award of CPAE Speaker Hall of Fame. You may contact her at (541) 994-3550 or 1825 SW Coast Ave., Lincoln City, OR 97367.

Gail Wenos is a member of the National Speakers Association. She has earned the certified speaking professional designation and was the recipient of the CPAE Speakers Hall of Fame award. She is a contributing author for *Meditations of the Road Warrior.* Her messages on teamwork and making a difference are heard by audiences throughout the U.S. Gail can be contacted at Gailnezra@aol.com or through her website at www.gailnezra.com.

Bobbie Wilkinson is a freelance writer, artist, musician, and songwriter, whose proudest accomplishments are her three grown daughters. She lives with her husband in a renovated barn in the northern Virginia countryside, where her favorite pastime is appreciating the beauty that surrounds her.

Steven W. Wise lives and writes in Columbia, Missouri, where he is co-owner of a real-estate appraisal firm. He and his wife Cathy have two children, Travis and Stacee. He is the author of three novels, *Midnight, Chambers,* and *Long Train Passing.* You may contact him at wisenovel@aol.com.